Her fingerprints are on the gun, but Sarah swears she's innocent.

Although Sarah Anne Martin admits to pulling the trigger, she swears someone forced her to kill her lover. Homicide detective, Jay Christianson, is skeptical, but enough ambiguous evidence exists to make her story plausible. If he gives her enough freedom, she'll either incriminate herself or draw out the real killers. But, having been burned before, Jay doesn't trust his own protective instincts…and his growing attraction to Sarah only complicates matters.

With desire burning between them, their relationship could ultimately be doomed since Sarah will be arrested for murder if Jay can't find the real killer.

I0675885

Books by Karen McCullough

The Detective's Dilemma

Published by Kensington Publishing Corporation

The Detective's Dilemma

Karen McCullough

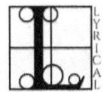

LYRICAL PRESS
Kensington Publishing Corp.
www.kensingtonbooks.com

Lyrical Press books are published by
Kensington Publishing Corp. 119 West 40th Street New York, NY 10018

All Kensington titles, imprints, and distributed lines are available at special quantity discounts for bulk purchases for sales promotion, premiums, fund-raising, and educational or institutional use.

Special book excerpts or customized printings can also be created to fit specific needs. For details, write or phone the office of the Kensington Special Sales Manager:
Kensington Publishing Corp.
119 West 40th Street
New York, NY 10018
Attn. Special Sales Department. Phone: 1-800-221-2647.

Kensington and the K logo Reg. U.S. Pat. & TM Off.
Lyrical Press and the L logo are trademarks of Kensington Publishing Corp.

First Electronic Edition: November 2014
eISBN-13: 978-1-61650-651-3
eISBN-10: 1-61650-651-2

First Print Edition: November 2014
ISBN-13: 978-1-61650-652-0
ISBN-10: 1-61650-652-0

Printed in the United States of America

To all the police officers who let me ride along with them and patiently answered my many, many questions.

Chapter 1

The crash of something hitting the floor jerked her awake.

Sarah lay for a moment, listening, wondering what might have fallen, but not yet alarmed enough to drag herself out of bed and investigate.

An even louder thunk shook the house. She jolted upright in bed. Something had hit the floor again--something heavy. She reached for the bedside clock and pressed the button to illuminate the face. One-thirty. Vince might still be up. Maybe he'd bumped into something. She hoped it was nothing worse. She kept telling him to follow the doctor's orders and lose weight. At fifty-three, he already had heart problems.

The thought of him lying on the floor after a heart attack or stroke goaded her up and out of bed.

She snagged her robe off the chair and rushed out of her bedroom. A light shone at the opposite end of the hall that ran nearly the entire length of the house. In the past year, Vince had been having more trouble sleeping and often stayed in his study, working or watching television into the early hours of the morning.

The door to the room stood open, but she didn't see him at first when she rushed in. Papers lay scattered across the floor, drawers hung open from the desk, and one sat on its side on the floor as well.

"Vince?"

"Over here. I--" His voice wavered and broke.

She spotted him on the far side of the room from the door. He was on his feet and two men flanked him. Hoods concealed their features, and they both wore dark, nondescript clothes. Each held a gun, one pointed at Vince's head, the other turned in her direction.

Sarah froze. Her breath stuck in her throat, and her stomach clenched into a tight knot. "What--? What's going on? Vince?"

His normally florid complexion had a gray cast, and his shoulders slumped. "I'm sorry, my dear. These gentlemen have--"

"Shut up," one of the two ordered.

She didn't realize there was a third man in the room until he stood beside her. Sarah backed away, but he grabbed her arm and held her in place. He squeezed the arm so tightly it hurt when she tried to wrench it away.

"Shut up." He lifted her arm from her side to chest height and pushed his gun into her right palm. Strong, square, latex-gloved hands flanked hers, holding her fingers around the gun's butt, pointing it toward Vince.

When she didn't put her index finger on the trigger, he tried to jam it into position.

"No."

She wriggled and twisted, but he kept such tight hold on her, she couldn't get free. Her stomach churned.

"What are you--?"

The hand on hers squeezed, pulling backward on the finger just touching the gun's trigger, then tugged again and again. Three shots exploded in rapid succession, one blast right after the other. The recoil pushed her back against the assailant's body, but he held her steady so that all three bullets found their target.

Vince jerked after each shot. Red splotches exploded on his stomach, his shoulder, and the side of his face. At a distance of no more than eight feet, even the assailant's shaky aim hadn't missed.

The echoes of the shots rang in her ears and shivered through her body. Her own screams blended with them as she scratched at her captor's sleeve with her free hand, struggling to get loose. A frenzy of panic robbed her of all clear thought and reason. The man let go and shoved her forward. She dropped the gun, stumbled to her knees, and dove across the room, expecting the impact of a bullet any second.

She scrambled behind Vince's desk and waited, her breath heaving in and out on harsh pants, but no one came for her. Footsteps retreated down the hall and a door slammed. Then quiet reigned, broken only by a low, rattling groan, which she heard even over the continued ringing in her ears.

As she crawled across the floor to Vince, her hand landed on a sticky spot, one of several spreading patches of blood staining the pale gray carpet.

He lay on his side.

"Vince?"

He opened his eyes. "Sarah? You're…?"

"I'm okay." The words came out on a sob. "I need to-- Oh my God! Hold on. I need to call 911."

"Wait. Need to…tell you. You have the key. You--"

He gasped on a series of shallow breaths and then closed his eyes and lay still.

She shook him. A sob tried to push its way out of her tight throat. "Vince!"

No response. She crawled back through the mushy blood-soaked spots on the carpet to the desk, where she levered herself up and grabbed the phone. Her hands trembled so badly she misdialed the first time. By the time the operator asked how she could help, Sarah could barely speak. Nausea roiled her stomach and waves of cold rushed up and down her spine. When words finally came, they poured out in an incoherent rush.

"Be calm, ma'am," the voice on the other end implored.

Sarah was beyond listening. She slid down the side of the desk, the phone receiver cradled in her trembling hands, until she heard the sirens approaching.

* * * *

Detective Jay Christianson surveyed the crime scene from just inside the door of the room. On the far side of a spacious office, the body of a bald, heavy-set man rested in a pool of red that soaked the plush carpet beneath and around him. The victim wore a navy polo shirt, khakis, and loafers. Blood spattered the far wall in two main blotches with sprays of smaller drops surrounding them. The smaller patches had started to dry to a rusty brown at the edges while more heavily drenched areas remained fresh and dark red. Dark spots disfigured the gold brocade drapes of the nearest window. A gun--the murder weapon, he presumed--lay on the floor to his left, near an immense desk of dark wood. A couple of overturned drawers lay beside it and papers littered much of the floor. He wrinkled his nose. A faint tang of gunpowder still hung in the air, beneath the nauseating smell that suggested one of the bullets had ripped an intestine.

The combination of money and violence guaranteed this case a high profile. Looked like he wouldn't be getting any sleep tonight. "Messy," he said.

Jay's partner, Sam Hennesy, shook his head. "Yeah."

While the evidence specialists took photographs and videotaped, the medical examiner waited his turn, along with the detectives.

The first cop on the scene stood at the side of the room, his complexion a bit green, but his eyes steady and serious. He was young, but he'd done the right things and was holding together. He'd do.

"You want to talk to the girlfriend while we wait?" Sam asked.

Jay didn't take his gaze off the body. "Where is she?"

"Next room," the young officer said.

"She saw the crime?" Jay asked. "She said so?"

"More than that. She said she did it. She shot him, but she said she was forced to. It's…bizarre." The officer shrugged.

"Go write it up. Right now, please," Sam said. "Her exact words to you."

The cop nodded. He led them to the next room down the hall, some kind of den, and then left without shutting the door. A young woman huddled in a chair. She was barefoot, with long, tangled dark hair, wearing a blood-stained robe. She looked young, early to mid-twenties maybe, pale, shaky, and very attractive, even with her hair a mess and no makeup on her tear-streaked face. Her dark eyes, wide but glazed, tracked them as they crossed the room.

"Ma'am?" Sam said.

Her eyes widened and her gaze focused on Sam. "He's dead, isn't he?"

Jay glanced at Sam, who nodded.

"Yes, ma'am. I'm sorry," Sam said.

She drew in a sharp breath, and a single tear slid down her cheek. She wiped it away, leaving a pink smudge, and looked up at them, her glance moving from one to the other. "You're police officers?"

"Detectives, ma'am," Sam said. He introduced himself and then Jay. "And you are?"

"Sarah Martin."

"Are you a relative of the deceased?"

"Vince. His name was Vince. No."

"You live here?"

She nodded. "I'm his-- Was his…companion."

"Companion? What does that mean?" Jay asked.

She looked up at him and shrugged but didn't say anything.

She's either in shock, none too intelligent, or very clever indeed. Jay's mental antennae began to vibrate. *She's certainly pretty and knows it.*

His hormones knew it, too. Even though she might well be a murderer. Christ. He suppressed the surge of anger along with the message from his groin.

As he met her gaze, though, something else inside him responded. She looked dazed, confused, and helpless. The stupid, gallant part of him that had failed to rescue Theresa woke, suggesting he had another opportunity to rescue someone in need.

No way. He wouldn't go there again. Not in this lifetime. He needed to focus on the case.

"Can you tell us what happened?" Sam asked.

She stared at them for a couple of moments, her gaze flicking between them. She took a deep breath and let it out slowly. "I was asleep. A noise woke me. I thought Vince might have… He had heart problems, you know. Anyway, he doesn't always sleep well, so I went to see if he was okay, and… There were men in the room with him. They had masks on, and they had guns. Another one came over to me and shoved a gun into my hand. He held it there, and then he pushed my finger onto the trigger and squeezed. The bullets… They hit Vince. The gun kept bouncing up, but the guy holding me dragged it back down. The noise… My ears are still… And the blood, the blood, everywhere. I crawled through it. I thought they would shoot me, too. I guess I panicked. I went to him and he tried to talk, but then he just went still. I guess he… He…" She shook herself and closed her eyes. Tears leaked out from beneath her lids, and she drew her knees closer to her chest. Her bare feet poked out from below the edge of the robe. A smear of crimson stained her toes.

Only her sob broke the silence that fell after she stopped talking. Jay looked at his partner, and the older man stared back at him. Sam shrugged. It was a damned far-fetched story, but it had the ring of truth. Of course, she might be one hell of an actress. He'd met some good liars.

"One of them pushed a gun into your hand and put your finger on the trigger?" Jay didn't quite succeed in masking his disbelief. "Why would he do that?"

She shook her head. "I don't know. I don't know why any of it happened. Why did someone want to kill Vince?"

"You don't have any idea?" Jay tried to force his tone to neutral and failed. The harshness remained.

She frowned. "He… His business, maybe. Some of it was…"

"Illegal?"

"I don't know about illegal. Maybe on the edge, though."

Jay turned to Sam again, checking for his reaction.

The other man's eyebrows rose. "What kinds of things--?"

A cop stuck his head in the door. "Detectives?"

The photographers must have finished. Jay told the officer at the door to stay with Sarah while he and Sam looked at the scene.

"What do you think?" Sam asked as they walked down the hall.

"Wildest story I've heard since that kid on the Ridge claimed his gun went off in his pocket and just accidentally killed three people."

"Still, she'd have to be a hell of an actress to bring it off."

"And who's to say she isn't?" Jay said. "Pretty young woman, 'companion' to a wealthy middle-aged guy... I bet she's been doing some acting."

"Open mind," Sam reminded him.

"Brain hasn't fallen out yet."

The medical examiner and an evidence specialist talked near the door of the blood-spattered office but looked up as Sam and Jay entered.

"What do you know?" Sam pulled a notebook and pencil from his pocket.

The medical examiner glanced down at the body before answering. "White male, late forties, early fifties, three entrance wounds, two exit wounds. Matching holes in the wall behind him. Won't be sure until the autopsy, but I'm guessing two of the three shots could have been fatal, one in the head, one in the abdomen. Third shot through the upper arm. Angle of the head wound says death would have been quick, if not immediate."

"How long ago?" Sam asked.

"Hard to be exact at this point. No *livor mortis* yet and very little cooling. I'd guess within the last couple of hours, but you know better than to hold me to anything at this point."

Jay nodded and turned to the evidence specialist.

"Got three shell casings and the gun, of course," the woman said. "Ten millimeter Glock. Eyeball says the casings match the gun. Blood spatter consistent with placement of bullets in him. Lots of blood on the floor, too, and a stream on the clothes suggests he didn't die right away but bled heavily for a few more minutes after he fell. There's a series of handprints going through the blood toward the body and then away, with some smearing, possibly from cloth dragging through it. And there's this." She moved to the left and pointed at the largest pool of blood near the body.

Jay stared down at the plush blood-splotched carpet but didn't immediately see what she meant.

"Right here on the edge." She indicated a fainter stain closer to the door. "It looks like someone might have stepped in the blood. And..." She moved a few steps over. "Traces of bloody footsteps going to the door." A rust-colored print in the shape of the back half of a shoe stained the gray carpet.

"Anyone here stepped in it?" Sam asked.

She shrugged. "No one admits to it. You'll want to check it out, but the pattern looks like a running shoe to me, size eleven or twelve most likely, and no one here's wearing them."

Jay did a quick footwear scan. He wore loafers, Sam wingtips, the M.E. deck shoes, and the other cops all had on uniform footwear.

"Do a shoe check on everyone who's been in the room since the call came in," Jay said.

She nodded. "Another thing. It gets fainter, but there are more traces in the hall, and they lead to a back door, not the one any of our people have used."

"Show me."

Sam snapped on a pair of latex gloves. "I'm going to look through the desk while you go."

Jay nodded and followed the evidence specialist. The blood trail grew fainter as they went, but unmistakably led toward a side door out of the house. "You'll need to check the knob, locks, and around the outside."

"Got a couple of guys on it already. I know my job."

"Sorry. Murder puts me in a bad mood."

She nodded. "Working all night does it for me."

He studied the knob and lock without touching it. "Locked, but the deadbolt's not thrown. Get a picture. Any sign of a break-in on the other side?"

"Not that we could tell. Be easier by daylight tomorrow."

"We'll want that report ASAP. I'm going to take a look at the body."

"Right."

"I'll need you to get the clothes from the girl and check her out. You swabbed her hands?"

The woman nodded. "Before you got here."

"Plenty of blood on her robe. Stay with her while she changes clothes?"

"You're taking her downtown."

"Of course." He went back to the office. Sam had gathered up some of the scattered papers and put them in a box. "Find anything?" Jay asked.

"Lots of homework. Name was Vincent Capelli, and--legally or not--he did pretty well. He wrote a monthly check for five grand to Sarah Anne Martin. The rest will take more digging."

Jay gestured toward the victim. Sam came around the desk to join him. They stepped carefully, avoiding patches of bloody carpet.

The body didn't tell them anything the medical examiner and evidence specialist hadn't already. The man had carried a lot of weight on a frame that probably stood only five eight or nine. Balding, jowly, with big ears and a large nose.

"Anything jump out at you?" Sam asked.

"It wasn't his looks that kept Sarah Anne Martin with him."

Sam's harsh laugh was half wry humor and half agreement. "I guess we're going to have to have a long talk with the lady."

Jay drew a deep breath and sighed. "Looks like a long night."

Chapter 2

The policeman who'd shown up at the doorway when the detectives went out stayed with her. Sarah shivered as the two men left.

Neither had come right out and said it, but they didn't believe her story. Their raised eyebrows and the awkward pauses between questions made their doubts all too clear.

Detective Hennesy was an older stocky man with a homely face moderated by a kind, sympathetic look in his eyes. He might give her the benefit of the doubt. The other man, Detective Christianson, was younger, taller, leaner, and would have been good looking except his expression was cold, almost harsh. No sympathy there.

"Are you all right, miss?" the young police officer asked. "Can I do anything for you?"

Can you make this all be a dream? She shook her head. "No thanks." *Vince, what the hell happened? Who were those men and why did they do it?*

Cold settled into her bones. Were they going to arrest her? What would she do then? She couldn't make her brain deal with it.

"Could I get a cup of coffee?" she asked.

The cop pulled out a box and spoke into it, asking if someone could get her the requested coffee. "We'll try to get some for you," he said.

Before it arrived, though, the pair of detectives returned.

"We've got to check every shoe in the place," Christianson said.

Hennesy ran a hand through his thinning hair. "Marcia's on it. Her guys are gathering them up."

"Good." Christianson turned to her. "We'd like you to come down to the office with us. We're not arresting you, but we have questions we need to ask. First, we'd like you to change clothes and give us what you're wearing."

A woman came into the room behind him.

"Why?" Sarah stood, hoping she could stay upright as dizziness threatened.

"Evidence," Christianson said.

The cold harsh tone made her shiver again. She looked up at him, meeting eyes whose color teetered between blue and gray but had ice in them either way. Still, for a moment she sensed something more behind those cool eyes, a fire he deliberately kept banked perhaps, a warmth he had to restrain.

She wanted heat. She felt stiff and shivery, like her bones were turning to ice.

"Ready?" the female police officer asked.

Sarah followed her out of the room. The skin on the back of her neck prickled. The detectives were watching her.

Sarah led the way to her own bedroom and crossed to the closet to get a pair of jeans, a shirt, and a fleece jacket. She got clean underwear out of a drawer and headed for the bathroom.

"Leave the door open," the other woman said. "And hand me the robe and gown when you take them off. They're evidence." She slipped on a pair of latex gloves.

Sarah stopped in the doorway. "Can I take a shower? I've got blood all over me."

"Not yet. I need to get some pictures of you dressed and undressed. Just to record the blood on you. And we may need more later."

Fortunately the woman was quick and took no more than a few seconds snapping the pictures. When Sarah had changed and handed the things to her, the woman put them in a bag, sealed it with tape, and labeled it.

"Ready to go?"

Sarah shrugged into the fleece jacket and pulled her purse out of a drawer. Was she ready? Not really. She wasn't ready for any of this. She felt like a robot or an animated ice sculpture. Her body moved, did the right things, but somehow her brain hadn't caught up. Emotions were on hold. She lingered in that moment between knowing an injury had happened and feeling the pain from it.

That numbness saw her through the trip to the police station with the two detectives, being escorted to a small room with nothing but a table, five chairs, and a mirror on one wall--probably a window from the other side--and filling out an informational form. She gave them phone numbers for Dan and Marc, Vince's sons. She didn't know his ex-wife's number.

"I want you to understand that you're not under arrest right now and you're free to go if you wish," Christianson said.

Right now? "You think I killed him."

Christianson's eyes narrowed.

Hennesy's tone and expression were gentler. "Miss Martin, you admitted you pulled the trigger on the gun. We have to start with that.

More ice congealed inside her. Even the blood in her veins was getting sluggish. Her brain wouldn't work. Dark stars gathered at the corners of her eyes and nausea roiled her stomach. A hand pushed her head down to her knees. After a moment in that awkward position the darkness retreated. She drew a deep breath before she straightened up.

"You want a drink or something?" Hennesy asked.

"Coffee, if I can get some."

Christianson left the room and returned a few minutes later with three cups of coffee, a few packets of sugar, and artificial creamer. It had to be the worst coffee she'd ever tasted, even with two sugars, but it was hot. She wrapped her hands around the cup and let the warmth penetrate her. Sipping it helped thaw some of the ice inside.

The first questions were easy--her name, address, birth date, and other facts about her life. Christianson tossed them at her, one after the other, while Hennesy scribbled notes on a legal pad. She answered with no problem, telling them she'd been born right there in Charlotte, North Carolina, the date, and her parents' names. It went smoothly until they got to her place of employment.

"I don't have a regular job." She watched Christianson's eyes for his reaction but they remained neutral. "I go to school. The community college."

"What are you studying?"

"Just got my GED four months ago, in June. I'm working on a transfer associate degree right now."

"You're twenty-five and still going to school?"

"My mom got sick and there was only me to take care of her, so I had to drop out of high school."

"What about your father?"

"Died in an automobile accident when I was eight."

"No other family?"

"My mom was an only child and her parents died a while back. I don't know about my dad's family. My mom never talked about them and we never heard from them, even when he was killed. It was always just the three of us."

"Three?" Christianson asked.

"My mom, me, and my younger sister, Barbara."

"Where is Barbara now?"

Sarah set the coffee cup aside and studied the fingers of both hands as she wove them together. "She's gone, too. About a month after my mom died, we found out Barbara had leukemia."

"Lot of bad luck in your life," Christianson said.

She looked up, confused by his tone. Sympathy or suspicion? His expression didn't help her decide. The frost still chilled his light blue eyes.

She shrugged, fighting the searing pain cutting into her chest. "And now Vince. It's not a good idea to get close to me." She sat up straighter. "Damn. Self-pity alert. I really try not to go there."

Hennesy said, "You've got some reason for self-pity, but you're right. It's better not to indulge it." Oddly, he threw a hard glance at his partner.

Did Christianson have something to pity himself for, too?

"That's what the therapist said." she agreed.

The younger detective narrowed his eyes at his partner, but his expression smoothed out again when he turned back to her. "To the matter at hand. How did you meet Vince Capelli?"

No mistaking the coolness of the tone when he asked the question or the slight edge of...disapproval? He had an interesting face. It would be appealing if he weren't so cold and judgmental. She shook her head and dragged her attention back to the question.

"About six years ago I started doing some modeling on the side...to make a little extra money. I'm not tall enough to really do it professionally, but a couple of local agencies sometimes needed help. I could do it in the evenings when my mom and Barbara were asleep. I can't remember exactly what it was, but I was doing a charity fashion show, and Vince was there. We got to talking, and he was, well, nice. Pleasant and easy to talk to, and understanding when I told him about my family problems. He said that sometimes he needed an escort to go with him to some social things he had to attend for business. He was divorced, and it would give him some status to be seen with a...a pretty young woman. He'd pay me for it. He had lots of money, but he was kind of lonely. He didn't actually say that, but I figured it out."

She couldn't bear to see their reactions, especially not Christianson's. She picked up the coffee cup again and swirled the liquid, staring down into the small vortex. "People won't believe it, but I...I liked him. I wasn't in love with him or anything, but he was nice to me, and he really was lonely. We went out together for a while. Then my mother died and Barbara got sick, and eventually I'd used up all the money we had for my mom's medical stuff. Some of the doctors and clinics wouldn't even see Barbara because I still owed them money for my mom. What could I do?" She looked up at them. "What would you do? I couldn't let my sister suffer if there was *anything* I could do."

"So you asked Capelli for help?" Hennesy said.

A lump formed in her throat. "I didn't ask. He offered. If I became his…lover, he'd pay all the medical expenses and give me an allowance. It meant Barbara could get the best medical treatments. When those failed, I could at least keep her in comfort to the end. Vince was wonderful." The obstruction thickened, and she looked at her coffee again. "He did more than just pay the bills. He helped me. He was a friend when I had no one else. It was a terrible time after she died. I'd lost *everyone*. I don't know how I would've survived it without him."

She sniffed and fought against the incipient tears before she dared look at them again.

Hennesy's expression was kind. Christianson's showed only a cool slice of suspicion. Fear lanced through the pain of her memories. Detective Christianson doubted everything. He probably thought she'd made up the three men and that she'd actually killed Vince. She might be arrested, go to trial, and go to prison. Or worse. Murder could get the death penalty. What could she do? How to convince them? She missed Vince with almost unbearable intensity already. She could've talked to him about it.

The truth. Just keep telling them the truth. It was all she had. That and herself. It had been enough, just barely. She brushed away the tears and straightened. "I'm sorry. Drifting into self-pity again."

"Self pity? Or just grief?" Hennesy asked gently.

His kindness almost broke her control. Her eyes burned, but she forced a smile. "Probably both."

Silence ensued for a moment before Christianson broke it. "Tell us again what happened tonight."

She went through it again. The images remained so vivid, they might have been branded on her mind. She remembered going into the room, Vince standing on the far side, flanked by the two men, the other one coming to her and shoving the gun at her. The kick after each shot. If the man in the mask hadn't held her steady, it might have knocked her over. The noise… Her ears still rang with echoes from the gunshots. The blood, all the blood, everywhere. With an effort, she pulled herself back together and finished the story.

When she stopped talking, both men stared at her. Doubt rolled off the pair so strongly she could almost see it. Then their questions came fast.

"The sound that first woke you. Can you describe it?" Christianson picked up his coffee cup and grimaced when he took a sip.

"A thump or a crash."

"Like a body hitting the floor?"

"Maybe. Or a chair tipping over. Or…now that I think about it, a desk drawer being dropped on the floor. But I don't know for sure. I couldn't tell."

"But you're sure of the time."

"I looked at the clock when I woke up."

They went through every single detail of her story, questioning, asking her to repeat things or explain or digging for more information.

Hennesy consulted his notes. "The two men with Vince when you entered the room. Did you recognize them?"

"They had masks on. No."

"Full masks? Were you able to see any parts of their faces? Their hair?"

"No. They were more like hoods. You know those things you pull down over your whole head."

"Ski masks?" Hennesy asked.

"I guess." She described the builds of the two men, the color of their eyes, shape of hands, the black sweatshirts and pants they wore with the hoods. Every detail of the room, the intruders, even what Vince said and did were taken apart, examined, and mined for anything that might shed some light on what had happened.

Vince's last words to her, that she had the key, particularly interested the detectives, though she had no idea what he'd been talking about or what it meant. They made her go through everything she could associate with "keys," try to remember anything Vince might have said before about them, even speculate about what he might have been hinting at, but none of it helped her understand. She couldn't begin to guess what kind of key it was, or even if he meant a real key or a metaphorical one, and she had even less idea what it might unlock.

"Can we look through your purse?" Christianson asked.

Sarah handed it to him. "Go ahead."

He upended it, but let things slide out gently, one at a time, onto the table. He set aside her cell phone, poked into the makeup bag, ignored the pack of tissues, sunglasses, and notebook, and glanced through the wallet. Then he picked up her key chain, holding it by the flat pen fob.

"Tell me what each of these keys does."

She identified the key to her car. The rest went to various doors around the house.

"No safe key or safe deposit box?"

"Nothing like that. I'm sorry. I really don't know what key he meant."

They went back to going through the events of the night. They spent what seemed like hours dissecting every sentence, almost every word of what she told them.

Then they switched gears and asked her about what she planned to do now.

"I haven't even thought about it. I want to go back to school. I need the degree to build a life. But…"

"But?"

"I'll probably have to get a job. I have some savings, but I don't know how far it will stretch."

"Savings? Won't you inherit something from Vince?"

Her tired, sluggish brain took a few moments to grasp the implications. "You think I killed him for an inheritance?" She started to laugh but felt it getting out of control and snapped her mouth shut. "His estate goes to his wife and sons. If he left me anything at all, it wouldn't be more than a small bequest. Vince liked me well enough, but I wasn't family. A mistress, maybe a friend, but not family."

"You didn't expect *anything* from him?" Christianson's eyebrows rose.

"He's already done a lot for me. He paid all the medical bills, and they were huge. He gave me a generous allowance, generous enough to let me build up some savings. I knew pretty much what was in his will. He told me. Everything goes to his sons except for a good-sized bequest to his ex. That seemed fair to me."

Christianson didn't say anything for a few moments.

So much for your theories that I killed him for the money.

Hennesy flipped a couple of pages of his pad. "Tell us about what he did earlier today. Anything unusual?"

She shook her head. "It all seemed very normal. I got back from class at four. He was in the office, working. I leaned in and waved like I always do. We had dinner at six. He went back to his office to make a few phone calls then went to the den to watch TV. I was studying in my room until about nine and then joined him. At eleven I went to bed, but he wasn't tired. That's it."

"He didn't seem worried or frightened?"

"No."

"Concerned about anything?"

"I don't think so. He didn't mention anything."

"Did he get any threats?"

"Not that I knew of."

"What did you argue about?" Christianson threw the question at her when his partner paused to write a note.

"Argue?" She hesitated, not sure what to say. "We didn't argue."

"You're sure?"

"Yes."

Christianson stared at her with those cold blue-gray eyes. "You never argued with him?"

"We had disagreements, yes. Nothing serious."

"What did you disagree about?"

"Politics, mostly. We have different views on some things."

"Money?"

"No. Or only once, when he wanted to buy me a car and tried to get me a Cadillac. I wanted something smaller and less…opulent." A headache gathered behind her eyes, running into her temples.

"What about your boyfriends? Did Vince approve?"

"What boyfriends?"

Christianson's eyes narrowed. "Come on, don't tell me a girl as pretty as you doesn't have a few male friends on the side. Or maybe just one special one?"

"No."

"Why not?" The questions came fast and hard, like hammer blows, making her head throb even more painfully.

"I… There was Vince."

"He owned you?"

"No, but I owed him some loyalty."

"You never spoke to any of the guys in your classes?"

"Well, I did occasionally."

"Flirted with them?"

"No."

"None of them ever asked you out?"

"Some of them tried, but I never accepted. And then word got around and they stopped asking."

"What word?"

He leaned toward her, his face only inches from hers. She couldn't escape being aware of him…large, threatening, and damn it, handsome.

Her breath caught. Pain, grief, and exhaustion wore at her control. "Because everyone at school knew. Knew that I lived with Vince. That I was his…"

"His whore?"

"Jay!" Hennesy shot out of his chair, glaring at his partner.

At the same time Sarah shouted, "His lover!" Tears threatened again and she swallowed hard and blinked, struggling to hold them back.

Christianson backed up a step but kept his gaze on her. "And that kept all the guys from making passes?"

"The rumor got around that Vince had underworld connections."

"Was it true?"

"I don't know. Probably."

Christianson took a longer pull from his coffee cup but his gaze never left her face. "You don't know?"

"Vince never said much to me about his businesses. He said the less I knew the better."

"Yeah, I'll bet."

She clenched her fists and fought for control, over anger this time instead of pain.

Hennesy glared at his partner again. "Jay."

Christianson drained the last of the coffee and crumpled the cup in his fist. Hennesy went back to making notes. "You know any of his business connections?" Christianson asked.

"A few." She rattled off the names of people she'd met at some of the parties or gatherings she'd attended with Vince.

"What about friends?"

"I don't know that he had a lot of close friends. The people I just mentioned are probably closest. And me."

"You?"

"We were friends."

"Let's go over it again," Christianson said."You went to bed at eleven. Did you go right to sleep?"

They wanted her to tell the whole story yet again? She glanced at her watch. Five-ten. She wouldn't be getting to class today, most likely. Especially not if they arrested her. She sighed and began talking.

This time Christianson didn't stop her as often but when he did, he was a lot more aggressive and hostile.

"You really expect us to believe someone actually forced a gun into your hand and made you shoot?"

"It happened."

"Stand up," he said.

Sarah complied.

The detective came around the table to stand beside her. "Which side did he approach from?"

"My left."

He walked to her left and stopped at her side. "I'm pushing a gun into your hand. Show me how he did it."

"He stood close to me, behind and on the left, and put his arm around me. He lifted my arm with his and pressed the gun into my right hand. He pushed his other hand against it too."

Christianson dug in his pocket, pulled out his badge case, and stepped closer until his side pressed against hers. It affected her in a stunning, shocking way. Awareness of him, not as a police detective, but as a man, crashed through her, sending a strange sizzle through her veins. Impossible. She shivered. He might be good-looking, but he despised her, or at least gave a good imitation of it. That didn't stop her body from reacting to his nearness. Prickles of awareness spread along her skin everywhere he touched.

He put an arm around her and lifted her wrist the way the killer had earlier. Mimicking the earlier scene, he stuffed the badge case into her hand and brought up his other arm. For a devastating moment, she was back in Vince's study with a crazy, dangerous man forcing a gun into her hand.

The shiver started at the base of her spine and spread upward. "No. *No!*"

"Calm down," Christianson said.

Hennesy picked up her coffee cup, brought it to her, and held it while she took a drink. It had cooled to lukewarm but still helped steady her as it settled in her stomach.

Christianson moved closer again and wrapped his arms around her. The position meant his body pressed against her back, and warmth from him penetrated through their clothes. She craved that warmth even as she recognized the danger of it.

He nudged at her finger, just as the killer had earlier. In pushing her hand against the case, he pressed on a sore spot. She gasped and flinched.

Christianson stopped.

"Are you all right?" Hennesy asked. "What happened?"

She looked at the finger. "I'm getting a bruise. Where he pushed my finger on the trigger."

Christianson stepped to the side, raised her hand and turned it so the light fell on it. He and Hennesy both looked. Neither could miss the dark smudge across the back of her finger. The men glanced at each other.

Christianson shrugged. "Let's get back to it."

They acted out the rest of the scenario. She told them about how their arms had jerked up with each shot, but the man had pulled them back down to point the gun again and squeeze her finger back.

Why did it feel good to have the detective's arm around her? That was so stupid. She didn't dare think about him as anything but an enemy.

He flinched when she moved. He pressed against her, and she felt the sudden tension that tightened muscles in his arm. Not just muscles in his arms. Proof that he wasn't entirely indifferent to her prodded at her lower back.

They finished the role-play of the scene. Hennesy stayed quiet for a few moments, his expression thoughtful. Christianson's blank look didn't give anything away.

A cell phone buzzed and Hennesy pulled it out of his pocket and answered. After a moment he looked at Christianson and nodded toward the exit.

"Evidence needs a DNA sample and we need to get your fingerprints for comparison," Christianson said as he followed his partner to the door. "I'll send someone in for you. We'll be back in a minute."

Christianson shut the door behind him.

Exhaustion made her sag in the chair. Her head throbbed and her body ached. She missed the warmth of the man's body. For a few minutes it had melted some of the ice freezing her, but the cold began spreading again. The uncertainty tormented her.

Were they going to arrest her for Vince's murder?

Chapter 3

Jay followed Sam into the hall.

"I'll need pictures of her hands," Sam said into the phone. "Marcia got some earlier, but the bruises might not have come out then. Make sure they're time-stamped. Right." He ended the call.

"What have they got?" Jay asked.

"Faint trace of a footprint on the walkway outside heading toward the driveway. Same print as the ones inside leading to the side door. No shoes in the place with a trace of blood on them except the ones the victim wore, none that match the print. No sign of a break-in, either."

"Not much. What do you think? Do we charge her?"

"It's a wild story, but she's consistent with it."

"She's smart enough to pull it off."

Sam frowned and shook his head. "Smart enough, maybe. But I don't think she's got the kind of ice-water in her veins it would take."

"She could have set it up. Maybe with someone who wanted him out of the picture. If he had mob connections, he had enemies too."

"Enemies who could have done this. They might have seen her as the perfect patsy. If she's telling the truth, they were making sure we'd have an obvious suspect and not look any further. In fact, if it weren't for the shoeprint, there wouldn't be much of anything to dispute it."

"It still seems too…unbelievable."

Sam stared at him for a second. "Jay, are you sure you're being entirely impartial on this?"

"What?"

"She looks a bit like Theresa."

"No."

"And she's a damsel in distress. You sure you're not fighting your inner white knight so hard you're leaning too far the other way?"

Jay clenched his hands into tight fists as he glared at his partner. "I don't believe this. The situations are totally different."

"Are they? Look, I understand. Theresa did a number on you. Nobody blames you. But you've got to know it's there and allow for it."

"You don't trust my judgment?"

"Not what I'm saying. Just saying that what Theresa did makes you distrust your own instincts about women, especially young, attractive women in difficult situations."

Jay froze in place, willing the anger to recede, forcing his body to relax before he throttled his partner. He rubbed a hand over his eyes. "I'm too tired to figure this out. What do you think about Sarah Martin?"

"My gut says she's telling the truth. She didn't waffle on the story or contradict herself. The bruise on her finger supports it too. She didn't even seem to know it was there until you pressed on it. There were a couple of others on her hand, if you looked closely. And there's no obvious motive. The will's too easy to check. She'd know there was no point in lying about it. Quick survey says she loses big-time with Capelli's death. Her sugar daddy's gone. And Capelli likely had the kind of enemies who could pull this off if they had a reason."

"I'm still not sure I'm buying it, but if we go with it, where does it take us?"

"Lots of homework."

"Hold her as a material witness?"

"Maybe we could." Sam tapped his chin a few times. "Those footprints make a pretty strong case for an intruder, unless we can find the shoe that did it. She gets a lawyer, she won't be hanging around long anyway. Don't see how we can prove flight risk except that she's got no family to hold her here. No place else to go either. I make it about fifty-fifty we get the warrant. But you know, we might get further if we don't try to hold her."

"Just let her go?"

Sam flipped pages on the legal pad. "Yeah, but one of us keeps a close eye on her. It might not have been just coincidence or convenience that someone tried to set her up for it."

"You don't think she'll run?"

"She was concerned about missing classes today. Doesn't sound like someone likely to light out. Anyway, she says she has no other relatives. Where's she going to go?"

"I suppose I know which assignment I get."

Sam laughed harshly. "Well I'm not the young, good-looking one here."

Jay rolled his eyes. "I doubt she sees me that way. Probably hates my guts by now."

"I expect it's more complicated than that. And you can change her mind."

"Even if I don't want to?"

"Are you sure you don't?"

"I wish you'd stop answering questions with questions."

Sam laughed. "Habit. Go play white knight, and then get some sleep. I'm going home and catch a few myself."

Jay nodded reluctantly. Sarah Anne Martin was a pretty young woman and all the more dangerous to him for it. He went back to the room where they'd left her and found it empty, but as he walked back out in the corridor, an evidence specialist came toward him with the young woman beside him.

"Done?"

The evidence guy nodded.

"Did you get the pictures of her hands?"

Another curt nod before the man departed.

"I'm heading out," Jay said to Sarah. "Where would you like me to drop you? Have you got friends or relatives you can stay with?"

She stopped and stared at him. "You're not going to arrest me?"

"Not right now. You got any relatives you can stay with for a while?"

"No. Can't I just go home?"

He shook his head. "The house is a crime scene."

"But… I don't know where else…" Dark semicircles smudged the skin beneath her eyes. She rubbed at a temple.

"There's a hotel not too far from here."

"I guess I'll have to, but I don't have clothes or anything."

"Why don't you go there and get some sleep, and I'll have someone bring you some things."

"Thank you. That's kind of you, Detective." She sounded exhausted.

He restrained an impulse to rub her tense shoulders and neck. She was a murder suspect. And he didn't do the white knight thing anymore. He'd learned his lesson about the costs of trying to rescue maidens in distress. Learned it the hard way.

Jay drove her to the hotel and waited while she registered to be sure he knew her room number. She had no car and very little cash so the odds she'd be going anywhere were slim, but he gave the desk clerk his number and asked him to call if he saw her leave. Then he headed back to his apartment to grab a few hours of sleep. It would be another long day.

* * * *

Sarah's cell phone buzzed almost as soon as she got inside the hotel room.

"Sarah?" Marc Capelli's voice sounded rough. "I just heard about Dad. I can't believe it. We're all stunned. Are you all right? Were you there when it happened?"

Marc, the younger of Vince's sons, was also by far the nicer of the two.

"Yes. I'm okay, but I just spent all night with the cops and I need some sleep."

"Cripes. They didn't arrest you or anything?"

"No. I'm not sure why not. I'm pretty sure they think I did it. In a way I did."

"What? What are you talking about?"

"I'm too tired right now, Marc. I'll tell you later."

"Okay. You need anything now?"

"Not at the moment."

She hung up and took a quick hot shower to wash off the blood before she crawled between the covers.

A pounding on the door woke her several hours later. She hastily donned the jeans and sweater before she looked through the peephole. A uniformed cop held up a badge so she could see it. Was he here to arrest her? Sighing, she opened the door a crack.

"Miss Martin? I've got some clothes and things for you." The young officer didn't linger after he'd handed her the rolling case from her closet. Someone had stuffed a random assortment of underwear, jeans, shoes, and tops into it, but it was enough. She took another long hot shower, washed her hair, and dried it with the hotel's dryer. By the time she finished it was after noon. She'd missed all her classes for the day.

She called Marc back and told him the entire story, including Vince's words about the key. He was shocked, of course, and outraged.

"The police do realize you're not guilty, right? They're out looking for the real culprits?"

Sarah sighed. "I don't know. I can't tell if they believe me or not. But I do think they're professional enough to investigate all possibilities."

"Poor Dad. I still can't believe it happened. It must have been hideous."

"It was, believe me."

"Why, though? I don't understand why anyone would want to kill him."

"That's the question. I don't think the cops have any idea, except that the intruders seemed to be searching for something. His office was all torn up."

"Any idea if they found it?"

"No clue. But... Maybe they did. Would they have shot him, if they hadn't?"

"Good question. God, I don't believe this happened. What did he mean about a 'key'?"

"I've no idea. I don't have any keys that I can't account for."

Marc drew in a long, deep breath. "Very strange. Any idea when they'll let us have the funeral?"

"You'd have to ask the cops about that."

"What are you going to do now?"

"I don't know yet. I'm just sitting down to think about it."

"Keep in touch," he said. "And if there's anything I can do to help, don't hesitate to ask."

She thanked him and ended the call. The enormity of her situation hit her then. She had just enough savings to cover two more years at the community college and another two at a state university, without living expenses, but no job, few friends, and no place to live. No Vince to help her with problems, to listen to her, to...

Grief surged over her and swept her away on a tide of weeping. Vince had been too young to die. No one should have his life ended so suddenly and brutally. The scene in his office last night... She squeezed her eyes closed against the memory, pressing until colored stars filled her vision. Those shots hitting Vince would fill her dreams for a long time.

After a while the worst of it calmed. She wiped away tears and splashed cold water on her face. She had things to do.

A pad and pen sat on the bedside table. Sarah picked up the pen and began making a list. She needed to start planning for a future that had taken a radical change of direction. A new place to live went at the top of the list. Some place cheap. She'd have to look at her savings, too, and figure out how far the money could stretch. If she were careful, she might have enough to pay for living expenses for this year plus pay the next semester's tuition before she had to find a job. That would get her halfway to the associate degree with enough left to cover her tuition for the next three years if she could find a job to cover living expenses.

Another knock sounded. She crossed the room to look through the peephole. Detective Christianson. She opened the door and stared at him, tamping down a surprising surge of excitement. Sunlight gleamed on his damp dark hair. A navy blue sport jacket showed off broad shoulders, and dark trousers encased long legs.

"You look better." He scanned from her hair to her shoes and back. "We'd like you to come back down to the station and help us sort out some of Vince's papers and things."

The detective looked better too. The tired lines on his face had eased and muscles in his jaw relaxed. The change made his expression warmer and less intimidating. That might be wishful thinking on her part. Or it might be an act on his.

"Are you arresting me?" she asked.

"No. Not yet. We want your help."

"You still think I killed him, though."

Christianson's mouth twisted into a grimace. "You pulled the trigger."

The reminder cut through her like a knife to the gut. She drew a breath and held herself rigid until she could control her emotions. She would *not* cry in front of this man. "Not because I wanted to." The words almost didn't get past the constriction in her throat.

"I--" He stopped and gestured toward the parking lot. "Let's see if we can figure out who *did* want you to, then."

Once in his car, she asked, "Do you have any leads?"

"We've barely begun to look into it."

"Oh. Do you have any idea when I can get back into the house? Not to live. I know it doesn't belong to me, and I don't have the right to live there anymore. But to get my things. And my car. The car is mine--I mean the title is in my name--and I need it to get to classes and to look around for a place to live now."

"I don't know about the house. It could be a while before it's released. I'll ask about your car. We might be able to get that back to you in a day or two."

"That long?" She sighed. "I guess I'll have to get the bus to class tomorrow."

His lips twisted in an ironic grin. "Most people are glad to have an excuse to skip classes."

"I can't afford to goof off, maybe even fail a class. Now more than ever."

"Why not?" He sounded genuinely curious rather than suspicious.

"Because I don't have anyone else to depend on. There's only me. Even before...before Vince died I knew I couldn't expect to live off him, forever. Eventually I'd have to depend on myself. That's why I've been going to school to get the GED for the last two years, and now I'm working on the associate degree. If I'm ever going to make something of myself, I've got to have an education. More than just the associate degree, too. I want a real college degree. You can't get a good job these days without it. My mom used to tell us that all the time. You can't get ahead in this world without the college degree."

"What will you do with it?"

"I don't know yet. Make myself into somebody."

"Somebody?" They stopped at a traffic light and he turned to stare at her.

She met his eyes for a moment. "Somebody who matters. A person who has a place in the world."

"You don't think you're someone who matters now? Doesn't every person matter?"

"Do I? When you first saw me last night, what did you think? Did you think, 'she might be someone with interesting opinions about things I might want to talk about, or someone who might do something important in the world?' Of course not. You saw me and thought, 'She's a rich man's pretty plaything. A parasite. And probably greedy enough to murder her lover for his money.' You did. I saw it on your face."

"Mostly I thought 'this woman was just involved in a murder and it's my job to sort out the facts.'" Christianson didn't say anything more for a moment as he turned the car into the parking lot of the police station. "You have a point, though."

"I know. You think I'm thrilled about it? When I was desperate to keep my sister comfortable, to keep us from ending up on the street--literally--I traded on the only asset I had. My looks. I don't want to be in that position again. Ever. I want to have something else the world values. A skill or knowledge. I'm not really smart, but I'm not stupid either. I just need the education."

He parked the car, turned off the engine, and looked at her. His lips relaxed out of the ironic twist and the lines around his eyes gentled. Not that his expression had softened particularly, but it didn't seem quite as condemning. Or maybe it wasn't as condescending.

"I don't think you're stupid at all," he said.

"It probably makes me more likely to have murdered Vince."

The man stiffened--an interesting reaction, though she couldn't guess what brought it on.

Finally he said, "I can't comment on that." He got out and walked around the car to open the door for her.

They went into the police station through a back entrance. He escorted her down a long drab hall and then into a room that held a dozen or so desks. Four of them were occupied, while several other people stood around or sat beside them. A couple of people spoke on the phone. Others talked to each other. The rumble of several different conversations and the constant buzzing of phones made her wonder how any work got done.

Jay led the way to a desk near the far corner, his apparently, since he sat in the chair behind it. She plopped down in the rough wooden seat pushed against its side. While most of the desks looked like a tornado had passed through the building, emptying file drawers and scattering the contents across every available surface, Christianson's was surprisingly neat. File folders sat in carefully aligned piles along the back and corners. A familiar book lay in the middle--Vince's calendar.

Several boxes stacked on the other side of the desk, against the wall, held the contents of Vince's filing cabinets according to the labels on them.

Christianson flipped through the calendar, got to the current date, which had no entries and began to work his way backward. He stopped frequently to point to a particular note and ask what it might mean, or to question who a first name referred to.

Some of them she didn't know, but she did identify several people Vince had met over the past few months and interpreted a few of the scribbled notes. While they worked, Sam Hennesy came in, said hello, settled in at the next desk down the row, and later came over and took a stack of folders from the top box. He sat and thumbed through them.

When he reached the beginning of the year in the calendar, Christianson flipped to the current date again and paged forward to check future scheduled items. Meanwhile, Hennesy occasionally leaned back and twisted around to ask her about things he found in the files.

Once he'd gone through the calendar, Christianson also grabbed file folders from the box.

They worked for a couple of hours. Both men occasionally stopped to answer the phone, but for the most part they kept reading through papers and questioning her about things they found. She had no idea if she told them anything useful or if they came on anything that might help identify the killers or who'd hired them.

Her cell phone rang somewhere around five.

"Sarah?" Marc identified himself. "I stopped by the hotel to see you, but you weren't there. Are you okay? Where are you?"

"I'm with the police. We're going through some of your dad's stuff."

At the last words, Christianson turned toward her.

"Any clues to who killed him?"

"Not as far as I know."

"I was thinking," Marc said. "If you need a place to stay, we've got a spare room."

"You know how Jeannie feels about me." Marc's long-time live-in girlfriend had hated Sarah from the moment they'd met.

"Yeah, but she'll lump it if I tell her it's happening."

"Thanks, but I'm going to look for an apartment."

"If you're sure. Let me know when you've found a place. Don't lose touch."

"Okay." She ended the call.

Christianson asked, "Which one of the sons was that?" The ice was back in his eyes and voice.

"The younger. Marc. He's always been nice to me."

"How did he feel about his father?"

"As far as I know they got along okay. The older brother, Dan, though… I don't think he ever forgave his father for divorcing his mother. And I was the icing on that resentment cake."

"Did he resent it enough to kill him?"

She rolled that possibility around in her mind. "It's kind of hard to believe, but I guess it's possible. I can't imagine why he would've waited this long, though. I've been…I was with Vince for three years."

Christianson scribbled notes on a legal pad. Once he finished, he got up. "I think we're done with this for the moment." He looked over at Hennesy. "Got any more questions?"

"Nope."

"I'll take you back to the hotel," Christianson said. "I'll see if I can get evidence to release your car. It may take a couple of days. Let me have your cell number and I'll give you a call."

She gave him the number and stood.

On the way home, he stopped at a fast-food sandwich place. "I'm hungry," he said as he pulled into the drive-through lane. "You?"

"Starving. I slept through lunch."

"Why didn't you say something?"

"I didn't realize it until just now."

In addition to his own food, he bought her a sandwich, French fries, and a soda. When she offered a five-dollar bill, he refused to take it and said he'd put it on his expense report. As they pulled out of the parking lot, she noticed a machine dispensing newspapers and asked if he could stop long enough for her to get one.

"I wouldn't have guessed you for a news junkie," he said when she got back in the car. He must have seen her expression change because he added, "Wait. This isn't about brains or knowledge. It's about interests."

She let out a breath and nodded. "You're right. I bought it for the classifieds and the rental guide. I need to find an apartment. Fast. And cheap."

"Most cheap apartments are in places a young woman should *not* be living by herself."

"You have a better idea? I don't have a lot of money to spend. Even if I get a part-time job, the only things I can do won't earn a whole lot."

"I'll ask around. But do me a favor. Check with me before you commit to a place. I'll tell you if there's a serious risk or not."

"All right. Can I get your number?"

After he'd turned into the hotel parking lot and stopped, he reached into his jacket pocket and pulled out a card. "The number's on here. Give me a call about the apartment. Also if you think of anything or come across anything that might relate to who wanted Capelli dead."

"I will. Detective..." She stared at him. The sun rested just above the horizon, its rays coming from behind and to one side, outlining him in a halo of light. For a moment, she saw the man and not just the police detective. Scary, because he was a damned appealing man. Handsome, but not pretty-handsome the way a few of the nicer looking guys in some of her classes were. More rugged-handsome, with echoes of his life already showing on his lean, angular face. The strong muscle, controlled expression, and the tense lines that bracketed his mouth hinted at a man who'd seen unspeakable things, had suffered personal setbacks, yet retained a fundamental strength and integrity. The sunlight also picked out a few silver threads in his dark brown hair, though she didn't think he could be older than his mid-thirties and was probably a couple of years younger than that.

This was scary and dangerous. The man likely thought her guilty of murder. She couldn't afford to regard him as anything but an enemy, which made his kindness all the more insidious. He might be doing it to get closer to her in hopes she'd somehow betray her guilt.

Yet... The way he examined her face, gaze lingering on her lips and cheeks, suggested some awareness on his part as well. And the slight twist of his lips indicated he wasn't any happier about the attraction.

A horn blared nearby, jolting them out of the distraction. His expression reverted to its professional remoteness.

"What time is your first class tomorrow?"

"Tomorrow's Friday? Nine."

"I'll ask tonight and see what we can do about your car."

Sarah reached for the door. "I hate to push it, but can I ask for one more thing?"

"What?"

"My books and papers and laptop. They're all in a bag in my room. I'll need them. I'm behind in my homework now."

"I'll ask about those, too."

"Thank you for supper and all your help." She opened the door and stepped out, closing it behind her.

He pulled out of the parking space as soon as she'd made it to the hotel room door.

Chapter 4

As she ate the sandwich and fries in the plain, lonely hotel room, Sarah studied the apartment listings in the classifieds section. After eliminating those she couldn't afford and some in places too dangerous, three remained.

One had already been let, she learned when she called the number given in the ad. The other two were still available. She made appointments to look at them on Saturday, hoping she'd have her car back by then.

With nothing else to do, she settled in for an evening of watching television. At a few minutes past nine, Detective Christianson called.

"You can get your car back," he said. "I'll pick you up at eight-thirty tomorrow morning. Someone from evidence will put your books and stuff in the back seat. It's the Accord, right?"

"Yes. Thank you!"

As promised, he showed up at the hotel just before eight-thirty the next morning and drove her to the house to get the car. Her backpack sat on the backseat and she got to her first class on time.

At lunchtime, Rob Helmond walked by with a tray, stopped, and asked if he could join her. Sarah nodded to the seat opposite.

She and Rob had shared a couple of classes the previous year. He was cute, pleasant, and personable. He'd tried to pursue her for more than friendship for a while but eventually got the message she wasn't interested and backed off.

"I heard about your friend," he said. "I'm sorry. It must have been terrible."

"It was."

"Are you all right?"

Sarah didn't want to encourage him to start pursuing her again, but she couldn't resist the temptation to talk with someone willing to listen. She told him what had happened and her fears that the police would arrest her.

He paid attention, offering words of encouragement, but did nothing more. When they finally parted to go to their separate classes, she felt better for having had that conversation.

That afternoon she found a free apartment rental guidebook and culled a few more possibilities.

On Saturday, she looked at apartments. The first two places she visited were hopelessly bad, one a damp basement with an unbearable odor problem. The second had broken windows, although the landlord promised they'd be repaired shortly, a refrigerator that didn't work, and a stove she'd be afraid to turn on. The third one had dangerously outdated electrical wiring in poor repair.

On the fifth try she found a possibility. It was in a two-story block of eight apartments that all opened onto a central hallway. The one she looked at was on the first floor at the back. The cost came in right at the limit she could afford. It was small and in need of fresh paint. But the appliances worked, the water ran both hot and cold, and the drains drained. Even better, if she put down a deposit she could move in right away.

Mindful of her promise, she called Christianson. "I think I've found a place," she said.

He didn't recognize the address and asked for directions to get there.

He arrived fifteen minutes later, wearing jeans and a polo shirt topped by a battered leather jacket. The rough clothes looked good on his tall, lean frame. Little butterflies fluttering in her stomach couldn't be attraction. Couldn't be. Shouldn't be.

"Are you off duty?" she asked, walking out to the hall to meet him. "I didn't mean to disturb your off time."

"I told you to call." He still wore the reserved expression that gave no clue to his thoughts or emotions.

She'd assumed it was his 'cop-face,' but it might be something more basic to the man.

"I was out running errands anyway." He looked around slowly. "Neighborhood's not great, but not terrible either. Okay for a woman alone as long as you're careful. Can I take a look at the apartment?"

"Sure, if you want to."

He nodded and walked with her down the short hall to the flat. The leasing agent eyed Christianson warily as he went to a window and looked out.

"I thought it was just you alone," the woman said.

"It is. I'm just checking the place out as a friend," the detective said. "The windows need locks. They're too close to the ground. You need a deadbolt on the door, too. And a peephole." He went off to check out the small kitchen and returned a moment later. "Wiring looks okay. Got a smoke detector. Overall, not bad."

"I'll go ahead with it," Sarah told the leasing agent.

"Let me go get the papers. I'll be right back."

When she'd left Christianson looked at her. "It's not what you're used to."

"Actually, it's not that different from before I met Vince. I can get used to it again."

She followed his gaze as he scanned the room. Dingy off-white paint on walls and trim, dirty windows, and scuffed, stained hardwood floor gave it a run-down air, but a bit of work would brighten it up.

He didn't comment on any of those things. "You don't have any furniture."

"I know. I figured I could get one of those blow-up beds for now. I'll check some used furniture places for a table and chairs. After that I'll take my time and see what I can come up with from yard sales and such."

"You're serious about this."

"Of course I'm serious about it. What else am I going to do? I've got to have a place to live."

He smiled, the first time she'd seen him do that, and those fluttering butterflies in her stomach began to dance. Not good. So not good.

"Why are you doing this?" she asked. "I'm betting most murder suspects don't get this much help from the cops."

The smile faded. She hated to see it go, but at least it lessened the danger to her.

He stiffened and retreated a step. "This isn't exactly a normal investigation."

"I figured."

"And if you're not the guilty party, you're another victim of the crime."

"Oh. I hadn't thought about that. I try not to see myself that way. Too easy to slide into…places I don't want to go." Places she sometimes went anyway, often late at night, when she desperately missed the family she'd lost and wondered why fate had singled her out for so much cruelty.

He gave her a harder look, but it wasn't so much condemning as searching. "How do you stay away from those places?"

"Sometimes it isn't easy. I try to stay busy. Exercise so I'm tired enough to sleep at night. Keep my mind occupied with other things. Now I have a life to rebuild. I hope that will keep me distracted."

His eyebrows rose for a moment and he turned to stare out the window. Since nothing was out there but a row of trees, she suspected he saw something else entirely. It gave her a minute to study him from the side. The lines of tension in his face and the shadows in eyes more gray than blue at the moment proclaimed he had places he didn't want to go, also. Maybe all cops did, or all homicide detectives anyway. So why did she think it might be something more personal that haunted him?

"It's a good strategy," he said, dragging his attention back to the present. "I'd better get going. Call me if you need to. I expect I'll be in touch."

"Thank you for the help."

He nodded. "Don't forget to get those locks."

The leasing agent returned shortly after Christianson left. Sarah completed and signed several forms, turned over her credit card information, and got a key to the place in exchange. She went back to the hotel to gather her things and load them in the trunk of her car. On the return trip to the apartment, she stopped at a big box superstore and got an air mattress, pots, pans, dishes, and enough canned goods to get by for a day or two.

As the evening went on, she thought of more things she needed and began a list. A lamp for studying. The overhead lights had low-wattage bulbs that made reading difficult. A couple of glasses for drinks. A place to hang her towels in the bathroom. Towels to hang, for that matter. The list grew rapidly.

She spent an uncomfortable night on her own in the apartment. She'd bought only one thin blanket. Since it was nearly the middle of October, the nights were chilly and apparently the heat in the place wasn't running very high. She'd have to call and find out if that could be fixed. Traffic noise into and out of the complex remained steady until the early hours. When she did sleep, she relived the shooting in her dreams.

The next day she ran into one of her neighbors as she got home from another shopping trip and wrestled several bags down the hall to her apartment. The door to the front apartment on the opposite side opened and a woman emerged. She wore skin-tight leopard-skin leggings with high-heeled boots and a leather duster. Hair dyed flame red fell in cascades of curls around her face, which bore a heavy layer of makeup.

The woman locked the door and turned to Sarah who was in the process of undoing hers. "Hey, you the new neighbor?" She sounded friendly, if a shade too loud.

Sarah turned to greet her. "Yes, Sarah Martin. I just moved in yesterday." She grimaced at the bags weighing her down. "Had to go get a few things. I'm pretty much starting from scratch."

"Oh, man. Did he get *everything*? Been there, done that. Doll, get yourself one of those high-flying lawyers next time and make *him* eat it."

It took her a minute to figure out what the woman was talking about. "No, I'm not divorced. It's more complicated than that, but the bottom line is I'm out on my own for the first time."

"Oh, well. I've probably got some extra stuff. Got more junk than I know what to do with, in truth. I'm Pam, by the way. On my way to the health club and then to work, but I'll catch you later."

Sarah settled in for an evening of trying to catch up on her work for class the next day.

Monday started pretty normally except that she had to readjust her mental schedule since her new location was farther from campus. Things started to get weirder after lunch break. A nagging prickle kept telling her someone followed her. Several times she turned to see who was behind her, but she never caught anyone watching or trailing.

On her way to the parking lot, someone called her name and she turned to find Rob just behind her. He looked flushed as though he'd been running and breathed heavily.

"Late for Econ," he said, "but I saw you and wanted to say hi and see how you're doing. You okay?"

"Hanging in," she told him. "Thanks for checking. Don't let me keep you."

He nodded and took off again, jogging toward a classroom building.

Sarah sighed and shook her head. She liked Rob but hated to encourage him.

As she drove home from classes, she glanced in the rearview mirror and spotted a dark blue car. The next time she checked the mirror, that same car had dropped a couple of lengths back, but then it made several of the same turns she did. Half a mile or so from the apartment, it faded farther back, and she lost track of it. When she swung into the apartment complex parking lot, she watched for it, but no one turned in after her. She wanted to see if the car would go by, but the dip and curve at the entrance hid the traffic on the street from view.

She debated calling Detective Christianson, but she didn't feel sure enough of the facts. And even if it had happened, what could he do about it?

She hadn't cooked for herself in a while, but she hadn't forgotten what little she knew, especially when supper involved opening a package and putting the tray and its contents into the oven. She needed to get a microwave, but that would have to wait. She wanted her television, too. How soon would they let her get her things from her old room?

The knock on the door came later, as she worked on homework again, lying on the air mattress, propped up against a pillow.

She needed to get a peephole. Most likely the neighbor she'd met earlier was bringing the things she'd mentioned.

Wrong. The figures in her doorway were familiar--sort of--but not people she'd ever wanted to see again.

The three men clustered in the hall wore jeans, jackets, and ski masks concealing their faces. Sarah's heart skipped a beat, and then jolted into a higher gear. She pushed the door closed again, leaning into it, but one man put a foot in the opening, while another shot out an arm and caught the door, forcing it back toward her. It almost knocked her over when they shoved their way into the room. She scrambled to stay upright. The last one slammed the door behind him.

Sarah backed up to the far wall. Terror had her pulse racing. She couldn't drag enough air into her lungs and barely got out the words, "Who are you? What do you want?"

"Where is it?" The man in the center asked. He had a deep, gravelly smoker's voice. "Where'd he put it?"

"Where-- Where is what?"

"Insurance. Where's the insurance?"

"What insurance? I don't know what you're talking about."

The man with the smoker's voice grabbed her arm and pulled her close. He reeked of tobacco and beer. "You know what we're talking about. Capelli said you had the key to it."

"I know he *said* so, but he forgot to tell *me* about it!" She tried to wrench herself free of his hold. "I don't know where it is. I don't even know *what* it is. I told the cops that, too." Her vision misted and stars floated on the periphery.

Tobacco-breath released her and nodded to his cohorts. One of them went into her bedroom. The other rummaged through her purse and pulled out her keys.

"What are these?" her captor asked.

"The one with the dark casing is my car key. This one next to it is for the apartment. The rest of them go to the house. Vince's." *This isn't happening. It can't be happening to her again.*

The guy fumbled with them, taking all the house keys off the ring and dropping them in his pocket. The ring, with its now lonely pen fob and car and apartment keys, he tossed onto the floor before he pawed through her purse. He unpacked her book bag. The thug stared at the laptop for a couple of minutes before he set it aside and tackled the side pockets of the bag. He looked around but found nothing else in the room to search.

He went to the kitchen and opened each of the four cabinets. "Geez," he said, after glancing in them and the two drawers. "She ain't got much of nothing."

The men returned to the living room shortly, shaking their heads.

"Okay, lady," Tobacco-breath said. "Let's get serious. We want that key."

They crowded in on her. Sarah's heart pounded so hard she feared it would burst right out of her chest. Pressure made her head feel like it might explode and her breath refused to work right. "What key? I don't have it. I don't know what you're talking about."

The man who'd searched her purse pushed her back against the wall. Her shoulder connected with a thud, and a flare of pain arced down her arm.

"You better think about it, girl, and come up with something." Tobacco-breath gripped her wrist and twisted to make his point.

She gasped as abused muscles protested.

"You think *hard*. We'll be back. You better have something for us."

The three left as quickly as they'd arrived. Sarah's head whirled with shock. Her knees wobbled, but she forced herself to go to the door and peek out. No one was in the hallway, so she crept along to the front of the building, hoping to get a glimpse of the license plate on their vehicle as they left. The men ran across the parking lot and jumped into a late model Chevy blazer, but the plate had some kind of reflective plastic over it. She couldn't read the numbers.

She went back to the apartment and locked the door behind her. Her hands shook so badly it took three tries to push in Christianson's number on her cell phone.

Chapter 5

Jay carried a cold beer from the fridge to his recliner, settled into it, and flipped on the television, looking for the Monday night football game. His cell phone buzzed just as he found the right station. He usually kept it nearby but he'd forgotten to move it to the table when he sat down. He sighed and forced himself to get up.

He recognized Sarah Martin's number.

"Detective?" Her voice shook.

In an instant he snapped from relaxed mode to alert.

"What's wrong?"

"Three men… I think it was the same ones that killed Vince. They came to my door and forced…"

"Shit. Are you all right? Are they still there?"

"They're gone."

"Lock the door and don't let anyone in until they identify themselves as a police officer. Understood?"

"Yes. I've locked it."

"Good. Stay with me. I'm going to the other phone and have the nearest patrol unit dispatched to you."

He picked up his landline phone and called in the request. Once that was done he went back to the cell phone. "Sarah?"

"I'm here."

"I'm on my way out the door, but there is a patrol officer on the way. He should be there in five minutes or less. Stay on the line with me. Okay?"

"Yes."

He snagged his jacket on the way out the door to the car. "Are you hurt? Did they touch you at all?"

"No. A couple of bruises maybe. One pushed me against the wall, and another one twisted my wrist, but I'm not really hurt."

"Damn it." He reached into his pocket for the car keys.

"They wanted to know where something was. The insurance. They called it that at first. Then they said I had the key. I told them I didn't know where it was, but I don't think they believed me."

She spoke too fast, stuttering and tripping over her words.

"Sarah! Calm down. Take a deep breath. Right now."

"Okay." The hiss of an indrawn breath followed, and then a huff as she let it out.

"Now another one. And another."

"All right," she said. "I'm calmer. Oh. There's someone at the door. He's saying he's a police officer."

"Hold on and let me check before you answer." He grabbed the radio and called dispatch to confirm there was a patrol officer at her door. "It's okay, Sarah. It's one of ours. Answer it, but leave the connection open. I'm about ten minutes away now."

"All right."

Clicks sounded as she opened the door followed by the murmur of voices.

He tried to concentrate on driving and failed.

Sarah Martin might have faked the intrusion to support her case and win his sympathy. She was clever enough to think of it. If she had enough nerve and acting ability to pull off the murder scenario, this shouldn't challenge her.

His gut said she was no actress. After the fiasco with Theresa, he no longer trusted his instincts about attractive young women.

Still, he rode the accelerator harder than normal and made it to her apartment complex in a total of twelve minutes. He pulled into a slot between a marked cruiser and an evidence truck.

An evidence tech he didn't recognize brushed the closed door for fingerprints. He flashed his badge at her and waited while she finished. The job took only a minute or two but he had trouble containing his impatience. He needed to see for himself that Sarah was all right.

Finally the tech finished and opened the door for him. He didn't recognize the patrol officer with Sarah, either, but the city of Charlotte, North Carolina had thirteen patrol divisions and more than fifteen hundred sworn officers.

She stood with her back against the wall, probably because she didn't have a damned chair in the place to sit on. He walked over and introduced himself to the cop but kept his eyes on her. She wore jeans, a sweatshirt, and no makeup. Her hair needed combing and her expression looked strained. In fact, she looked damned beautiful. He fought an urge to pull her into his arms. When she turned to him, relief spread over her face. He moved right in front of her--too close, but he didn't care and she didn't object.

"How do you feel?" he asked.

"Okay." She ran a hand along her wrist, where a bruise already started to darken.

"Tell me what happened."

She pointed to the officer. "I just finished telling him all about it."

"Are you done?" Jay asked him.

"Yes, I think so. Unless there's something else you want to add?"

Sarah shook her head. "No. I've told you everything."

"I'm done too," the evidence tech said, while packing equipment and samples into a bag.

"Will you be all right, miss?" the officer asked.

"I'm going to take her to the hospital to get checked out," Jay said.

"I'm fine," Sarah protested. "I don't need to go to the hospital. It's just a couple of bruises."

"Humor me. I want to be sure."

She hated to have to say, "I can't afford it."

"I'll make sure it's covered. You can tell me what happened on the way."

"All right."

The patrolman and the evidence tech left.

"You'll want a sweater. It's cool out there," Jay said.

She nodded and took a moment to get one before they left.

He helped her into the car and started it. "Tell me what happened." He checked for traffic and pulled out of the parking lot.

"There was a knock on the door. I don't have a peephole or a window where I can see who's coming. Anyway, I was kind of expecting a neighbor I met earlier, or I probably wouldn't have opened it. They had masks on. I'm pretty sure they were the same ones who…killed Vince. It looked like the same masks." She told him how the men had pushed their way in and searched her place. "Of course, that didn't take them more than about ten minutes."

It wouldn't have, not in her bare, empty apartment.

"Then they kind of crowded around me, and this one pushed me back against the wall, and they started asking me questions." She related those to him as well.

"Insurance?" he repeated. "You're sure he said insurance?"

"I'm sure. And he said, 'Capelli gave you the key to it.' I told him Vince hadn't told me anything about it, and I didn't know where it was. I guess he sort of believed me, because he told me to think about it. Hard." She pushed hair off her face with both hands. "I wish I had some idea, but I'm clueless. I don't like the feeling."

"What about your things still in the house? Could he have given you something that had a key hidden inside it?"

"I've been trying to think of something. I guess there could be a key hidden inside of something, but he never said anything about it."

They pulled into the parking lot of the hospital. Things moved fast after that so it was a while before he had time to talk to her again. They both filled out paperwork, and an aide came and took her back to an examining room. He settled into the waiting room with two or three other people and thanked whatever powers had charge of such things that the TV was tuned to the football game. Around half-time, a nurse brought Sarah out.

She smiled at him. "I'm fine, just like I told you. Couple of bruises, nothing more."

The nurse nodded. "X-rays were negative and there's no sign of serious injury. Might be a good idea to keep some cold packs on those bruises to reduce the swelling."

The distrustful part of him said the bruises were convenient and easily induced. The other half wanted to introduce the thugs to his fists and make them very sorry they'd touched her.

They checked out and got back in his car. Sarah remained silent for a while before she asked, "Do you have any idea when I can get my things from the house? It's not a lot, but there are a few things I'd like to have."

"I don't know. Probably in a few days. I'll let you know. I'd like to look at anything Vince gave you. That thing about 'insurance' interests me. We didn't find anything in Vince's files that would incriminate anyone else, though there's plenty to suggest he dabbled in less than legal stuff. There were some things that were obviously missing, too. Papers that should have been there. So what did he do with them? If someone thinks you have them or know where they are, it puts you in a dangerous position."

"Tell me about it."

"Tomorrow I'm getting in touch with a guy I know who does security. What time do you get back from your classes? I want him to come look at your place and tell me what we can do to secure it."

"My last class tomorrow ends at two, but I have a paper due in a week and I still need to do some research in the library." She grimaced. "This is more important. If he needs to come earlier, I'll put it off."

"Good."

When they got to her apartment, he walked with her to the place and checked it out to be sure no one waited inside.

Saying goodbye proved awkward. He still fought the urge to pull her into his arms and kiss her. Those wide dark eyes of hers, shadowed with sadness and fear, brought out all his protective instincts. His 'Inner White Knight' Sam called it. Her looks, the nicely rounded figure and perfectly shaped breasts tantalized other more earthy and direct parts of him. His jeans became uncomfortably tight. He had to resist it, though. Getting involved with her in any but the most professional way was wrong. He offered a nod and a curt goodbye.

He cursed himself for a fool as he got back in the car and headed for home. Sarah Martin filled his mind and drove his hormones crazy. He couldn't stop thinking about her, worrying about her, wanting her. But she was still a prime suspect in a murder investigation, which made her way off limits.

The fantasies refused to go away. He could picture her snuggling up against him, what she'd look like as he undressed her, and... Oh, hell. He didn't need this. He'd been there before and the scars still ached sometimes.

He called Brad Nayland as soon as he got into the office the next morning. The man agreed to meet him at Sarah Martin's apartment at three that afternoon, bringing tools and locks.

Unfortunately Sam was in the office as well. His partner's head popped up when he heard Sarah's name. "What's that all about?" he asked when Jay hung up.

"Guys broke into her apartment last night. Might have been the same ones she says were there the night Capelli died."

"They try to hurt her?"

"Roughed her up a little. Not much. Seemed more like they wanted something they thought she had. Demanded to know where the insurance was. Or the key."

"Key? Interesting. How did they know about it?"

"Good question. I don't know. Unless Capelli told other people that she had it. I suppose that was his insurance. He hid some damaging material somewhere and gave the key to her. But she didn't know she had it, and maybe that was deliberate on his part too."

"SOB left her in a hell of a dangerous position if that's the case."

"No kidding," Jay agreed. "If it isn't all an elaborate lie."

"What do you think?"

"Haven't decided yet. Find out anything interesting yesterday?"

Sam cocked an eyebrow and gave him a wry grin before his expression went serious again. "Not much. Got the phone records from both Sarah's cell phone and the house phone. Nothing interesting on Sarah's--mostly calls to the house. A few calls and texts to other students here and there about assignments or meeting for lunch. Nothing to connect her to a murder conspiracy. House phone didn't give us much more. Helped me track down three more people named in his records. Only one seemed like a good candidate, but he was out of town until day before yesterday and can prove it." Sam sighed. "Biggest problem we got here is that if Sarah Martin didn't engineer it all herself, those were hired thugs and we have to figure out who hired them. So far I don't have any good candidates, but that may be starting at the wrong end. If they're planning a return visit to her..."

"We set a trap for them?" Jay leaned back in his chair. "Baited with Sarah? I'm not really happy about that idea."

"If she's telling the truth, it looks like she's bait whether you or anyone else likes it. And by the way, when did you start caring?"

"She's a citizen. One of those people we're sworn to protect."

"Unless she's a murderer."

Jay froze and dropped the pen he held onto the desk. "Killer or victim, staying close to her seems like the best shot at solving this."

"True. Just don't get too carried away with it."

"How freakin' likely is that?" he snapped, irritated by the conversation.

Sam swiveled his chair around to face him square on. "I don't know. Do you?"

"What does that mean? Yeah, I'm trying to keep in touch with her. As you so wisely pointed out, she's our best link to the killer--one way or another."

"Let's hope it works out. Sergeant stopped by last night to say he would *really* like to get some closure on this case."

"Hell. Anyone left to track down?"

"Not really. I got some work to do on a couple of other cases, too."

"That's it for now, then."

At two, Jay got the autopsy report and agreed they were ready to release the body. The report didn't tell them anything they didn't already know. Capelli had died from the bullet wound in the abdomen. It had nicked an artery, and he'd bled out within a couple of minutes. The head wound would've been fatal a few minutes later anyway. The only other injuries he'd sustained beside the bullet wounds were a couple of bruises on the side of the face, where the intruders probably hit him.

Jay left the office at two-thirty. When he pulled up outside Sarah's apartment, he called to let her know he was there but would wait for Brad to arrive before he came in. The other man showed up minutes later and he rang her again to let her know when they were outside the door. She still opened it tentatively and released a long breath when she saw him there.

Brad looked the place over, came to pretty much the same conclusions Jay had, and set to work installing locks on the windows and a deadbolt and chain on the door. He finished by drilling through the door at her eye level and installing a peephole.

"Always look through the peephole first," Brad warned. "Don't depend on the chain. It's too easy to kick in a door that's just on a chain. If you don't know who's there, don't answer." He scanned the room and shook his head. "Fact is, even all this won't keep a good pro or even a persistent amateur out. It just makes it harder. I usually advise a young woman living alone to get a dog. Best thing there is for scaring off intruders."

"A dog? I don't think the complex allows pets."

"Think about it anyway," Brad said. "Doesn't have to be a big one, as long as it barks when someone tries to get in. Or there are motion detectors that reproduce the dog barking sound. Might be a good idea for you."

"I will think about it." She reached for her purse. "How much do I owe you?"

"It's a favor, miss," he said. "Jay's done a couple for me." He handed Sarah the keys to the new lock and the deadbolt before he departed.

"If you want you can return the favor to me," Christianson said, forestalling her as she turned to thank him again. "Call Marc Capelli. His father's body's been released. I want to know if they've made funeral arrangements yet."

She nodded and made the call, speaking to the man for a few minutes, and then thanking him.

"Thursday at ten at St. Luke's," she said. "Interment right after." She frowned at the phone once she'd ended the call.

"What's the matter?" he asked.

She looked up at him. A ray of afternoon sunlight pouring in the window cut across her face, illuminating her richly brown eyes. Even in the glow, though, sadness and worry shadowed them.

"I don't know. It just doesn't seem quite right for him to have a church funeral. He never went while he was alive. And… I don't know."

"He wasn't what you'd call a good man, was he?"

"I don't know. He wasn't an all-bad man either. He could be generous. He was always pretty nice to me. Of course, under the circumstances, I guess that wasn't much of a virtue. And he could be pretty cruel to the boys and Christine."

Jay sighed. "I don't know what to tell you. But we're not supposed to judge."

"No." She sniffed and held herself stiff for a moment. "I miss him. I liked talking to him. I feel…kind of empty right now. Like there's a big hole in my life. Nothing there."

"You're grieving. And still recovering from the shock. Give it some time."

She nodded, reached out, and took his hand.

He sucked in a sharp breath as the warmth from that contact headed straight for his groin.

"Thank you for everything. You're a kind man, Detective Christianson."

He reversed the hold so that he clasped her hand in his and squeezed, just a little. Anger made him want to squeeze even harder but he resisted. "Sarah, you should keep this in mind. I'm not a kind man. I'm a cop. Remember that."

She stared at him for a moment. "What does--? Oh." She jerked her hand loose.

The pain and anger in her eyes made his gut burn, but he had to do it.

"Anyway," she said as he left, "thank you for everything. Whether you did it out of kindness or…or something else."

He cross-examined himself during the drive home. Why had he done that? If he wanted to stay close to her to solve the Capelli murder, why warn her off? An attempt at brutal honesty? When she got over the hurt, she'd probably respect it. But it wasn't the real reason. He forced himself to look deeper. The truth was he was afraid of her and of himself. He feared the temptation she represented.

He didn't hear from her at all the next day and didn't see her again until the funeral on Thursday morning.

He and Sam got to the church half an hour early, wearing dark suits to blend in with the service people. They'd brought a photographer with them, who set up in a discreet corner to get pictures of the attendees. After a few minutes, people began to file in and take seats. Jay recognized many of the faces as belonging to individuals they'd interviewed in connection with the case. Others they recognized were more of a surprise.

He hadn't expected to see one of the mayor's staff or two city council members, since nothing they'd found in Capelli's records suggested any connection. No business connection, anyway. That puzzled him until he remembered that Sarah had met Capelli at a charity event. That might or might not explain the presence of the president of a small regional bank and the chairman of a somewhat larger industrial parts manufacturer as well. Plenty of people he didn't recognize had come too, which would mean hours spent later trying to attach names to the faces.

Sarah arrived ten minutes before the service started. She spotted them right away and nodded before walking up the aisle to take a seat by herself about five rows back. The conservative navy dress emphasized her slender build and elegant carriage, but it also made her complexion paler, giving her an air of fragile self-possession.

Moments before the service started, the family--Capelli's ex-wife, two sons, the older son's wife and two children, plus the younger son's girlfriend--filed in and filled the first two rows of pews.

Nothing remarkable occurred during the service. The bland impersonality of it fitted the fact that Capelli hadn't darkened the doors of the place for years before his death. After it was over, people filed out to their cars. The motorcade to the cemetery extended for most of a city block. Jay and Sam, in Sam's car, joined the procession.

They'd been driving for a couple of minutes when Sam broke the silence. "Jay…"

Jay knew his partner well enough to recognize the tone. Jay wasn't going to like what came next.

"Do we need to transfer this case?" Sam asked.

"What the hell? What brought that on?"

"You know damned good and well. I watched you watching her in the church."

"So? She's a suspect. I watch suspects."

"Not like that, you don't. You watched her the way a man watches a woman he's interested in. Maybe even involved with. It could get us burned."

"Hey, it was your idea I should keep an eye on her."

"I didn't mean for it to go any further that."

"Two nights ago, after I got the new locks put in her apartment, she tried to take my hand and thank me. Yeah, it made me sit up and take notice. She's damned good looking. You know what I told her?"

Sam raised an eyebrow.

"I reminded her I was not a kind man. I was a cop." His hand clenched into a fist. "She's smart. She got the implications."

"And?"

"It hurt her, and I felt like a heel. But that's the way it is."

Sam braked as the motorcade slowed to go around a corner. "You believing her story now?"

"Still not sure."

"Okay. You know, she's either a basically pretty nice girl who's had some really bad breaks or an incredibly ruthless, manipulative woman with Oscar-level acting talent."

"Vote?"

"Choice A," Sam said.

"I'm leaning that way, too," Jay admitted. "But I'm not ruling out B entirely."

"Can't," Sam agreed. "Which is why you need to be careful. You're walking a fine line with her. You've been the department's golden boy, making detective at the ripe old age of thirty-two. You're good. And the strategy is right. But you're human and--intentionally or not--she's pushing your buttons."

"I know. I'm keeping it in mind."

"Keep me in the loop. Okay?"

"You got it."

The day had started off cold, but the sun warmed temperatures into the mid-sixties by the time they got to the burial ground. The breeze carried the promise of winter in its chill and an elegy to summer in the smell of fresh-cut grass. Jay buttoned up his suit jacket.

Sarah hung back when the rest of the family and mourners crowded around the casket, her distance all too symbolic of the gap between her and Capelli's family. She looked lonely and vulnerable, yet at the same time strong and self-contained as she stood on a slight rise, some ten feet away from the others. The combination tugged at something inside Jay, a pull he resisted for all he was worth.

Rigid tension froze her body. She held a crushed tissue in her right hand and twice raised it to her face. She might be the most genuine mourner there. Capelli's ex-wife and two sons watched with almost no expression at all. That stone-faced denial of emotion could be the way they dealt with

grief, but in his interviews with them, he'd gotten no sense that any of
them would miss the man.

No one invited Sarah to come closer. They all ignored her until it was
over and the crowd dispersed. Capelli's younger son, Marc, went over
and said a few words to her. She nodded and took his hand for a moment.

Dan Capelli, the older brother, watched the interaction with a
contemptuous sneer twisting his mouth. His mother also glared at the
pair, making no effort to hide her animosity. The older woman's eyes and
lips narrowed even more when Marc pulled Sarah against him for a brief
embrace.

Sarah stayed behind, waiting until everyone else had gone but Sam,
Jay, and the people waiting to lower the casket into the grave. She walked
over to the elaborate box and put a hand on it for a moment. Her head
bent forward and a tremor shook her. She raised a tissue to her face and
swiped at her eyes.

Her chest rose and fell as she turned and walked away, heading back to
her car. Halfway down the gentle hill to the parking lot, she stumbled and
fell to one knee. He and Sam both went to her and helped her up.

"Are you hurt?" Sam asked.

Tears smudged her cheeks and the breeze blew strands of hair across
her face. "No, I'm okay, thank you. I wasn't watching where I was going."

"Will you be all right driving home?" Sam put a hand under her elbow.

They flanked her as she walked to her car.

She swiped her eyes again before opening the car door.

Jay wanted to insist on going with her, but he felt sure she'd refuse. It
would create logistical problems anyway, so he didn't push it. Before she
got in, he said, "Evidence is releasing the house tomorrow. I've talked to
the lawyer. The family insists he be there when you get your things. He
thinks they'll probably want to be there themselves."

She huffed a harsh, humorless laugh. "Are they afraid I'll steal the
silver? Or maybe take a box of tissues that doesn't belong to me?" She
got in the car and yanked the door closed. It was the first time he'd heard
any hint of bitterness from her.

She turned on the engine and drove off.

He suspected some of her bitterness was directed at him. And maybe
she had reason to feel that way.

Chapter 6

Sarah needed distraction, so once the funeral was over she headed back to campus. After grabbing lunch in the cafeteria, she holed up in the library, delving into research for the paper due next week. Burying herself in work might stave off the pain of losing Vince, the anger at his family, and the irritation with Detective Christianson.

It would catch up with her later, but maybe by then she'd be in better shape to handle it.

She actually did get distracted by tracing the antecedents of the Pre-Raphaelite poets. By the time she emerged from the library at six, a nice stack of index cards provided plenty of material to work with. The satisfaction of having accomplished that helped balance some of the pain and anger remaining from the funeral.

That evening, she made the rounds of a few grocery stores, collecting boxes for the move. After her last class ended the next day, Friday, she drove to the house she'd shared with Vince. Funny. A little over a week ago it had been home. No more. Now it was a place she'd once lived. The place where Vince had died. She waited for the sadness or regret to come, but it didn't--just a vague and surprising repulsion for the house and all it represented. She had to force herself to go inside again.

It already had the musty odor of disuse, with a hint of the coppery scent of blood and a darker note of…something nastier. The lingering smell of death, maybe.

The lawyer waited inside when she arrived, talking with Detective Christianson. She'd seen Craig Winthorpe a couple of times at charity events.

He shook her hand in greeting. "Sarah, I'm so sorry to meet you again under these circumstances. Who'd have thought? And I understand you were there. It must have been horrible."

"I'll see it in my dreams for a long time to come," she said. "Vince…
He didn't deserve that. I hope the police find out who killed him and see
that they're punished for it."

"Have you made any progress?" the lawyer asked Christianson.

"I can't comment on an investigation that's still in progress."

"Of course."

Further discussion was forestalled by the arrival of the Capellis--ex-
wife Christine and both sons. Marc came over and asked how she was
doing. The sympathy in his dark eyes upset her control and nearly set her
crying again.

She covered the effort to hold back tears by dropping her car keys in
her purse. "Doing okay. I'm coping. It still feels like a big hole in the
center of my life, but I'm starting to figure out how to work around it."

He turned on the smile that made her wonder why she'd never felt any
sexual attraction to him. Maybe because she'd been his father's lover,
so he seemed almost like a step-son? Yet he really was an attractive
man, with his easy laugh and dark good looks. He'd always been kind to
her, trying to mitigate the way his mother and brother either shunned or
vilified her. She liked him, but it had never gone beyond that. He had an
almost insanely jealous live-in girlfriend, so it was just as well.

A fine irony that the man who did attract her, who made her blood fizz
when he got near, was a police detective who probably thought her guilty
of murder. A man who'd warned her not to mistake his manipulative help
for kindness or any other interest. It did sometimes seem like fate had it
in for her.

Christine Capelli looked from her to the lawyer, Winthorpe, and
nodded to him.

The man huffed a bit and looked at Sarah. "I've been asked to remind
you that you have the right to take only what actually belongs to you,
things you owned prior to moving in here, you bought yourself, or that
were given to you as gifts by Vince Capelli. You have no claim on most
of the furnishings or other items in the house."

Sarah sucked in a sharp breath but kept her expression neutral. *I won't
let them get to me*, she promised herself. She even managed a credible
attempt to deflect their pettiness with humor. "It takes a lawyer, a cop, and
three family members to guard the fort against *me*?"

"Sarah, it's not like that," Marc said. "I came to see if you needed
help."

She stared at him for a moment. "I'm sure I can use it."

Marc flushed and nodded. She looked pointedly at every other person in the room, but none of them seemed either affected or abashed by her remarks.

Ignoring them all, she went out to the car and collected a stack of boxes. Marc followed and grabbed a load of them too, lugging them in behind her. To her surprise, Detective Christianson also toted a share.

She led the way back to her bedroom. The others joined her as she walked down the hall. The door to the office was shut and she felt no inclination to go in. Nothing of hers should be in there anyway. In fact, almost everything she owned was in the one room.

She went to the closet, taking the largest boxes for clothes.

"You can start loading books," she suggested, waving Marc over to one of the bookcases.

"It's probably going to take at least a couple of trips from here to my apartment," she told the others. "My car's not that big and it's going to be tough fitting the bookshelves and some of the other things. I should have hired a van, but it didn't occur to me."

"You can load some stuff in my car," Marc said.

"Give me a minute." Christianson pulled out his cell phone and pressed a couple of buttons. "Will? You got some time? Did you drive the Tundra today? Good. Could you make a side trip when you get off work? Probably about an hour... I know. You can blame it all on me."

He listened for a minute and a hint of a smile brightened his eyes. A complete change of expression hovered just beyond the crinkle at the corners of his eyes and around his mouth. It left her breathless and frightened. She might not want to see beyond his stiff and cold demeanor. It could threaten what little peace she'd been able to recover.

"Lisa never manages to stay mad at you anyway," he said. "Tell her I owe her another rose bush. See you."

He ended the call and said, "My brother has a pickup truck. He gets off work in"--he consulted his watch--"half an hour or so. Said he'd come on over."

She stared at him. The man just kept confusing her. One minute cold as ice and warning her not to read too much into his kindness, the next minute again going beyond the call of duty to help her. The almost-smile he'd worn earlier while talking to his brother had faded, but his expression hadn't gone completely back to its more habitual coldness. She wished she understood him better.

When she thanked him, he shrugged it off and looked at his watch again. She took the hint, moved to the closet, and began to take clothes down, stuffing as much as would fit into a rolling suitcase, the rest into a large box.

She emerged from the closet to find Dan Capelli going through her file cabinet. "What are you doing?" she asked.

Eyebrows rose as he looked up from a folder he riffled through. "Making sure you're not taking away any of my father's papers."

Heat burned in her face, and anger raced through her blood. She snatched the folder from him. "Mr. Winthorpe, would you mind checking through--"

Christianson interrupted. "No need. We went through those files last weekend. There's nothing there that concerns your father's business or your family."

Sarah stuffed the folder back in the file cabinet, keeping her face averted until she had her emotions under control again. She wasn't sure if she felt better or worse for the detective's words. Best to ignore it for now. On the bright side, he would have seen verification of what she'd told him about her family.

Because she wanted to get it done as quickly as possible, she began to drop things into boxes, making no attempt at neatness or organization. The entire contents of her closet were packed and ready to go by the time Christianson's brother arrived.

The newcomer was a shorter, older, more muscular and more personable version of his brother. The detective introduced them all to Will Christianson, and the man nodded at each of them until he got to her. He studied Sarah a bit longer, but he did it with a comfortable, lazy grin. "You're the lady who's moving?"

She nodded. "I appreciate your help. It's awfully nice of you."

His smile offered a tantalizing hint of what his brother could be like if he would lose some of the grimness. "Jay promised Lisa another rose bush. I'm golden. For a few days, anyway. So what's going? We want to load the biggest stuff first."

"The bookshelves, the escritoire desk and chair, the computer desk, and the filing cabinet are all mine. So is the small dresser in the closet."

Christine Capelli walked to the escritoire and ran her fingers over the burnished finish. "This is an antique, isn't it? Are you claiming Vince gave it to you as a gift?"

Sarah's hackles rose again but she kept her voice calm. "It was my grandmother's. One of the few pieces my mother and I couldn't bear to part with. The dresser was mine as a child and I bought the bookshelves and computer desk myself. Oh, the television and radio are mine, also. I bought those as well."

The older woman's lips twisted into an ugly frown.

Sarah refused to buckle under the disapproval and returned what she hoped was a steady, firm challenge. "I've got the receipts for them, if you don't believe me. In the filing cabinet. And I've got an old letter from an antiques dealer to my mother about the desk, too."

"I don't think we need to go that far," the lawyer said.

Christine Capelli's eyes narrowed. Dangerous lights brewed in their depths, but she remained quiet while Will, Marc, and Jay took the smaller dresser and drawers out to Will's truck.

The woman prowled around the room, peering into the empty closet, opening built-in cabinets, even going over to the large dresser and opening the jewelry box. She took out a pendant rimmed in sparkling stones. "Is this yours, or just borrowed from Vince?"

"He gave it to me. The stones are zirconia, not diamonds."

"And this?" She picked up a pair of pearl earrings.

"They were my mother's."

Christine dropped them back into the box. Instead of retreating, though, she pulled out a drawer from the big dresser that would stay and began flipping through Sarah's undergarments.

She lifted out a silk camisole."Did my *husband* buy this for you?"

At least the Christiansons and Marc were out of the room.

"Mother!" Dan Capelli put a hand on her arm.

The lawyer said, "Mrs. Capelli, you were divorced."

Sarah overrode them both. "Those are *my* things and you have no right to go rummaging through them."

Marc and the Christianson brothers returned while the woman still dangled her camisole.

Sarah snatched it from her and stuffed it back in the drawer. "I would appreciate it if you would leave the room. Your sons can make sure I don't take any knick-knacks or dust bunnies that don't belong to me."

"I think you do need to retreat, Mom," Dan said.

"What's going on?" Detective Christianson asked.

"My mother isn't dealing very well with the situation," the older of her sons said. "I think she needs to get out of the house for a bit."

"She's a thief." The woman glared at Sarah as both of her sons tried to guide her out of the room. "Don't leave her alone. Not even for a second."

Sarah clamped her lips shut against the nasty words she wanted to say. If she could make it through another hour or so of packing, she should never need to see the woman again.

Marc and Dan pulled their mother out into the hall. Sarah refused to let her feelings show on her face as she dumped the contents of the big dresser's drawers into boxes.

Marc returned a few minutes later. "I'm sorry about Mother," he said. "You didn't deserve that. She's under a lot of strain. I think Dad's death has hit her harder than we expected."

"You don't have to make excuses for her." Sarah finished retrieving the sweaters from the bottom drawer and put the last pile into a box. "Or apologies."

Will and Jay started moving the desk toward the door.

"You got any extra blankets we can use to wrap this so it doesn't get banged up?" Will asked.

Sarah looked at Marc. "Can I borrow a couple of blankets? I'll make sure to bring them back."

The man rolled his eyes. "For heaven's sake, take as many damn blankets as you need. I don't want them back. Nobody *cares* whether we get them back. I'm giving them to you. You can have everything in the room as far as I'm concerned." He looked at the lawyer. "I can do that, right?"

"Well, technically, it-- Oh, heck, yes."

"Thank you." He turned back to her. "Sarah, you can have whatever you want in the place. You want some of the furniture? Take it. Take whatever you need."

"You're a doll," she said. "But the truth is, I don't want any of it. I just want the things that are mine. Things that were in my family, given directly to me, or I bought myself. Everything else... I need to start fresh. I'm building a new life. It's better this way. I'm going to be better."

The Christiansons took the spread off the bed to wrap the desk and disappeared down the hall with the piece.

"Sarah, while they're gone..." Marc sighed and scratched his head. "Be careful. That detective. He's... He's not someone you should be getting involved with."

"I'm not involved with him."

"Maybe not, but you're not indifferent to him either. I see it when you look at him. And he's not indifferent to you. But he won't let that get in the way if he decides you might be guilty. He's dangerous to you."

"I know that. And I know better than to let myself get carried away with thinking he's some rescue ranger, come to help this fair maiden off a mountain or whatever. He's good-looking. And sometimes unexpectedly kind. That's all. He's too hard and cold to interest me."

Marc gave her a wry grin. "I don't think he's as cold as you think, but he hides it well. Anyway, just be careful around him. Stay away, if you can. He's nothing but trouble for you."

"I know that."

"Good. I'm sorry to be interfering in your life, but you know I think of you as…kind of a sister. I don't want to see you get hurt."

"I understand. And I appreciate it. More than I can tell you."

The others returned, and Marc went back to taking her own supply of linens and towels out of a cabinet and packing them up.

Three quarters of an hour later, they'd stowed everything in boxes and loaded them into either the truck, her car, or Detective Christianson's car.

When they went out the door, a group of reporters clustered on the driveway. *Where had they come from?* The men had done all the toting so she hadn't stepped out and seen them until then. *Why hadn't they warned her?* She debated ducking back into the house and asking someone else to drive her car away. That was a coward's way, though. She had to face this.

Detective Christianson came to her rescue again. He moved to her side and guided her through the crowd and into her car. "Don't say anything," he advised. "Ignore them and don't answer questions. Pretend you don't even know they're there."

Cameras whirred and microphones hissed as the reporters tossed questions at her, questions she saw no point in answering. Several reporters jumped into their vehicles and attempted to follow them as they drove off.

Moments later her cell phone buzzed.

"We're going to get rid of the tail," Christianson said. "If we split up, they won't be sure who to follow. Will and I will lose any of them that go with us. You try to do the same if any of them tail you. Make a couple of sudden turns close together, without signaling, do a U-turn if you can and then another turn, anything to get rid of them. We'll meet at your apartment."

"All right."

Will, who was behind her, turned right at the next available spot. At least one of their followers went with him. Another one changed his mind and turned to go back that way as well. The detective veered off to the left at the next traffic light, taking another vehicle with him.

Afternoon was fading into twilight, making it harder to see who stayed with her. She turned left herself half a mile farther on. The car directly behind stayed with her. The one behind it didn't, but another vehicle also turned.

She drove on for a few minutes, and her parade marched along with her. Two traffic lights later, she made an abrupt left turn, barely getting across in front of an oncoming truck so that her pursuers would have to wait. She hit the accelerator hard.

Less than a quarter of a mile beyond, she turned right again, just as one of her pursuers zipped across the intersection. Luck favored her. Another traffic light changed to yellow as she approached, and she took a quick right again. An older strip of shops lay on her right with a parking lot in shadows beside it. She ducked in, pulled into the farthest corner, killed the lights and motor, and waited.

One car drove past. She couldn't tell whether it had been following her. After a few minutes another car pulled into the parking lot, but its owner got out and went into the one store still open, a drug store.

Five minutes later, she started the car again and drove back out onto the street. No other vehicles lay in wait and no one followed her. She wove her way back to the main street and proceeded to her apartment unaccompanied.

Will was already there, sitting in the truck. With him escorting her, she got out and unlocked the apartment door. They retrieved boxes from the truck's bed, lugging them into her new home. He looked around the place when they brought in the first load.

"Wow, you really are starting from scratch."

"Pretty much. We all have to start somewhere, right?"

"Guess so."

Jay arrived ten minutes later.

"Got one that was damned hard to shake," he said.

They spent the next hour emptying Will's truck and their cars. When everything was in her apartment, Will took off, leaving her and his brother surrounded by boxes.

The detective looked around for a minute and shrugged. "I'm hungry. You up for take-out Chinese?"

"You're bringing it here? We'll have to eat on the floor."

"We'll spread out one of those blankets Marc Capelli let you use and have a picnic. Anything you don't like?"

"I don't like it very hot. Spicy hot, I mean. Otherwise I'll eat pretty much anything."

By the time he got back, she had most of her clothes hung up or squeezed into the drawers of the small dresser. Fortunately, the closet in her bedroom had shelves on one side where she could pile the excess.

They spread out a blanket in the living room and set out the containers of rice, shrimp and broccoli, sweet and sour chicken, pepper beef, and a handful of egg rolls.

Sarah surveyed the spread. "I hope you've got a really big appetite. It looks like enough food for a week here."

"You can reheat the leftovers for dinner tomorrow."

Fortunately, she'd washed the dishes after breakfast that morning, so she had two clean plates, forks, and spoons to contribute as well as a pair of clean glasses. "I've only got soda, apple juice, or orange juice to drink. Or tea, if you prefer that?"

"Soda's fine." He levered himself down to the floor, folding his long legs to one side.

Ignoring the flutters in her stomach, she poured drinks and sat while he took rice from one carton and bits from each of the others. He put aside the sets of chopsticks the restaurant had included.

"You ever tried to use those?" she asked, watching him.

"Tried, failed, wore the shame for the rest of the day." He picked up a fork. "You?"

"I've tried, but I can't seem to get the hang of it. Vince could, though. He'd spent some time in the Far East in the military. He tried to show me but I'm too uncoordinated. Actually he wasn't great with them, but he got more food to his mouth than on his shirt."

"More than I managed," Christianson said. "I think it's something you have to grow up doing to really get good at it."

"Like riding a bike?"

"Or dancing."

"Do you?" she asked.

"Dance? Not if I can help it. I'm not into public humiliation."

"I think you could be good at it."

"The world will never know."

Jokes! He made jokes. The man did have a sense of humor.

"What are you good at?" she asked.

The food was delicious. It deserved more attention, but her companion was taking the lion's share of that. The tight muscles around his jaw and eyes had eased, making him look less stern and more relaxed. He didn't smile, but his expression wasn't as hard and cold either.

"Police work. Puzzles. Figuring things out. Being persistent. Shooting."

"Shooting?"

"Marksmanship. I have several awards for it."

"Have you ever…?"

"No. Never had to. Hope I never will."

She nodded. "What else are you good at?"

He shrugged as he forked a floret of broccoli into his mouth and chewed. After he swallowed, he said, "Running. Dribbling a basketball."

"You played basketball?"

"In high school. Wasn't anywhere near good enough to be recruited by a college, and I wanted to go to UNC anyway."

"Did you?"

"Yup. Your turn. What are you good at?"

She used the excuse of chewing a mouthful of sweet and sour chicken to give herself time to think. "Me? Not much. I think I'm pretty good at schoolwork. I'm getting good grades, anyway. I'm good at taking care of sick people, but I'd rather not do any more of it. I'm pretty good at working with computers. I sort of understand how they do things. Not much else."

He set down his fork and watched her with a steady gaze. "I think you're probably good at a lot more things than you realize. You just haven't had the chance to find out yet."

"Maybe. I'd like to find out lots of things. I know some things I'm not good at all."

"What?"

"Sports. I'm a complete spaz, totally uncoordinated. Can't hit the ball in baseball, can't hit the basket in basketball, and let's don't even talk about dodge ball."

"Definitely let's don't talk about dodge ball. My least favorite activity ever." He grinned.

He actually grinned, and oh heavens, it was awesome. Sparkles glittered in his light eyes, making them warm and bright. And he had dimples. On one side, at least. His grin was a bit crooked, so the crease only appeared on the left, but it transformed his face.

It did wickedly dangerous things to her pulse and her breathing. This was so bad, so dangerous. She was so attracted to him. Worse yet, she liked him. But she was just a suspect to him. Or maybe not. He maybe liked her a bit, too, but he had to fight it. He couldn't let himself do anything else. She looked down at her plate, pushing food around until the excitement subsided.

"Sarah?"

When she looked up the grin had faded

He set his fork and the container of pepper beef down. "What's wrong?"

"A lot of things. You're being nice again, and I'm scared I'll take it the wrong way. And I'm realizing… Everyone thinks I killed Vince. That's why the reporters followed me. I'm the obvious suspect. And I don't know how to change that. What will it take to convince everyone I'm not guilty?"

His lips thinned as his jaw muscles clenched. "Probably the only thing would be for us to arrest someone else."

"I know you can't really tell me, but do you even have any other suspects?"

He froze into tense stillness. "All I can tell you is we're working on some leads."

She heard what he didn't say. He didn't expect those leads to go anywhere, and he didn't have anything better.

What could she do?

He might have been reading her mind. "It would help if you could figure out what Vince meant by the key. Or what insurance your thugs were talking about. That might tell us all we need to know." He picked up the container of sweet and sour chicken and spooned another helping onto his plate.

"True. I wish I had some idea where to start. I guess there's no point in going through the files since you already did."

"It's still worth doing again. You might spot something odd that we wouldn't even notice."

"True."

"Another thing. Did Vince ever give you gifts? Other than money or the car?"

"Sometimes. Small things. A jacket I liked. A stuffed teddy bear once when I wasn't feeling well. A few mugs with interesting designs on them. A music box. Stuff like that."

"While you're unpacking, set aside anything Vince gave you directly. I'd like to look over every gift. The smallest things--knick-knacks, jewelry, anything you didn't buy yourself."

"You want to start now?"

He took a last bite to clean his plate, unwound himself, and stood up. "Not tonight. I'm too tired, and I think you are, too. I'm on duty tomorrow night, but I'll come by in the afternoon, if that's okay with you?"

"Tomorrow's Saturday."

"Cops work all sorts of hours."

"Even detectives?"

"Crimes don't limit themselves to business hours."

"I know."

He extended a hand and helped her up. To her combined delight and dismay, he didn't release her as soon as she was on her feet. He didn't say anything for a moment. She looked at him, studying the hard lines of his face, the elegant cheekbones and jaw, the glitter in his light eyes, the spark of something he tried hard to control. She should move away, get back from the flames. But she couldn't. The heat of his gaze held her paralyzed and fascinated.

Without releasing her, he reached up with the other hand and touched her hair, running his fingers along the length of one strand down to her shoulder. His expression gentled as he swished the strand between his thumb and palm. He twirled it and brushed the ends across her cheek. "You have beautiful hair." He leaned forward and bent as if he might kiss her, but he stopped and the glitter in his eyes faded. He let her go abruptly and stepped back. "I'm sorry." He shook himself, like someone trying to shoo away a bad dream. "I had no right."

She tried not to be hurt, to see it from his point of view. For him, doing anything like that with her, a suspect in an unsolved murder, was wrong. "It's all right. We've all survived the experience." Why had she put that little edge of sarcasm on the words?

"Doesn't make it right," he said. "I shouldn't have."

"And if I didn't mind?"

"You should. You should be screaming at me and kicking and complaining."

"Kicking? Uh-uh. I've got enough problems without adding assaulting a police officer."

It helped dispel some of the tension.

He drew a breath so deep his chest heaved up and down with it. "I'd better be going." He swallowed hard and left, reminding her to lock the door behind him.

That night, before she fell asleep, Sarah indulged in a bit of fantasy about loving and being loved by Detective Jay Christianson. The kiss that almost happened would've been warm and hard and... Excitement prickled along her skin and made her stomach turn somersaults. His arms would gather her close, so close she could feel his heartbeat and he'd hear the way her breath got short. His lips would dance along hers and sparks would ignite on their surface...

When she fell asleep and began to dream for real, he appeared again. Only he wasn't kissing her.

He put handcuffs on her and told her she was under arrest for murder.

Chapter 7

Jay berated himself for a fool the entire drive home. He didn't need her to kick and scream at him. He handled that himself.

No matter what he believed about her, she was still a suspect in a murder, the most likely suspect. He couldn't get involved. However pretty she was, however much he liked talking with her, enjoyed her sense of humor, found touching her nearly irresistible, he had to resist.

Getting involved with a suspect wasn't just career suicide. It was wrong--even if he no longer really believed she'd committed murder.

After a couple of beers and an hour of *SportsCenter*, he finally got to sleep. The next morning he ran his normal five miles and took care of chores before he showered, dressed, and drove to Sarah Martin's apartment.

A sixty-ish woman with carefully curled gray hair and leathery skin sat on a lawn chair in Sarah's living room when he got there. The woman stood up. "Your boyfriend?" she asked, shooting a sly smile toward Sarah.

"Just a friend." Sarah introduced him to her neighbor, Emily Petrie, without mentioning he was a police officer or detective.

The woman nodded and shook his hand, giving him an appreciative stare that went up and down his body. "Nice to meet you." To Sarah, she added, "I'd better be going. Lots to do today. It was lovely chatting with you. Keep the chair for now. You need it more than I do."

Sarah thanked her and said goodbye.

"Mrs. Petrie lives in the apartment opposite," Sarah said when she'd closed the door. "She's a widow and seems kind of lonely. But nice. She brought some muffins she made. Want one?"

"No thanks, I just had lunch." He looked around the room. She'd done a lot of unpacking and sorting. Her antique desk and chair were set up between a pair of windows on the outside wall. The television sat on a low stand in the corner, and the bookshelves stood against an inside wall with the computer desk between them. A couple of shelves held rows of textbooks. The other bookcase held an eclectic assortment of books, boxes, and knick-knacks.

"I put all the things that were gifts from Vince over there," she said, following his line of sight to the bookcase. "There were more than I realized. He…" She stopped, and her shoulders slumped for a moment, but she straightened sharply. "Nothing made me think of a key."

"Tell me again what Vince said to you about it. His exact words if you can remember them."

"Those words are engraved on my mind. I'll never forget them. He said, 'You have it. Key.' He started to say something else, but he couldn't get it out."

"'You have it.'" *What had Cappelli meant by that?* "Can you remember any previous conversations where this might have come up? Anything he said relating to a key?"

She stood for a moment, staring at the wall, eyes unfocused. "I just can't remember a time when it ever came up, other than when he gave me the car key. But that wasn't any big deal. As I recall, he just handed it to me."

"We should probably go through your car. It's possible he hid something there."

She nodded. "Now?"

"Why not?"

She got her key ring and they went outside. She unlocked the car and checked around the back while he popped open the trunk, looked around, pulled up the cover and searched the spare tire compartment. Nothing unusual there. He went to the front of the car, trying to avoid staring at the enticing curve of Sarah Martin's hip as she leaned into the car and reached under the seat. He couldn't resist a couple of peeks as he opened the front hood and took a glance at the engine.

Mind on duty. He was looking for a key. *Avoid distractions.* She was a hell of a distraction in tight jeans and a sweater that kept riding up, offering enticing flashes of smooth skin. *Mind on duty.* He glanced over the engine, didn't see anything that looked like a key, and slammed the hood back down, harder than necessary.

Thinking there might be a magnetic key holder somewhere, he ran his hands along the inside edges of bumpers and wheel wells. The effort collected nothing but dirt. He straightened up and looked at Sarah, who snapped shut the door of the glove compartment. She turned to him and shook her head.

"I've been thinking," she said as she led the way back into the apartment. "If Vince meant for me to have a key, he wouldn't have hidden it any place too hard to find."

"True." Jay turned on the water in the kitchen to wash his hands. "But it would also be a place where no one else was likely to stumble on it."

"That could still be almost anything I owned."

"We're assuming he was talking about an actual physical key. It's possible it was something else entirely."

"Something more metaphorical? Like what?"

He shut off the water and dried his hands on a towel. "I don't know. Like the key to a code. Or the key to a location where he hid something? Maybe even a word or name."

Sarah shook her head. "It doesn't seem like something Vince would do. He wasn't fanciful. At all. He thought poetry was silly. A card on Valentine's Day was as poetic as he got. He didn't even like science fiction movies or shows. He preferred things to be real. He once said he'd been told he had no imagination. That was pretty much true."

"You're betting there's a real key."

She nodded as she opened another box and began to unpack books. "Of some sort. Everything I've come across that Vince gave me is on the shelf over there. I've looked at all of it and I didn't find a key in any obvious hiding places."

He started on the top shelf with a stack of books. They were mostly expensive, over-sized, high-gloss tomes that included a lot of photography. Many were books of art and architecture, including several on the construction of various monuments and grand buildings around the world. "Which one of you was interested in architecture?" he asked.

"Me."

He thumbed through one of the books, noting how much technical detail it included. "Are you interested from the artistic or engineering side?"

"Both. That's the real fascination. How to employ the mechanical in service of the artistic."

"Are you going for a degree in Architecture?"

"I was thinking about it, but it's a hard course and takes a long time. I don't know if I can afford it. What are you doing with that?"

He looked up from the book. "Feeling along the binding to see if anything might have been hidden in it."

"If it is a real key Vince somehow left me, what would it be to?"

"I've wondered that, too," he said. "There's a safe in his office, but it's got a combination lock and we found the combination in a box in his bedroom. Is there another safe you know of? We searched the house pretty thoroughly."

"Not that I'm aware of. Doesn't mean there isn't one, but if you guys didn't find it, I'm betting there isn't. You know, Vince does have a beach house down at the coast. I doubt he'd hide anything valuable there since it gets rented out when he's not using it, but it might be worth looking."

"We did. We found the paperwork in his files. Sam took a crew down to check the place out, but it was clean. My working guess right now is that any key would go to a safe deposit box."

"That would make sense. Wouldn't I have to have a signature card on file to access it?"

"You've never signed one?"

"Not that I know of."

"Could he have slipped it in when you were signing other papers?"

"Maybe when I did all the stuff for the car. It did seem like there were a lot of things to sign, and he was in a hurry that day so I didn't read everything very closely."

"So it's at least possible. And most safe deposit box keys are flat, easy to hide."

"Like in the binding of a book?"

"Like in the binding of a book. Unfortunately it doesn't seem to be in any of these." He set down the last in the stack and opened a polished wood box with a gold catch. It held several pieces of jewelry, a couple in classy silk bags. He opened each and let the contents slide out onto his hand, a silver chain with a blue stone wrapped in silver wire dangling from it, a gold chain with what looked like diamonds between some of the links, and a bracelet of several interwoven gold chains. He glanced in each bag, but none held a key.

Other pieces lay in the box, but none of them could hide a key. He checked the bottom, sides and lid, but all appeared solid with no place for a secret compartment. Beside the jewelry box lay an assortment of mugs with designs from famous pieces of art, Van Gogh sunflowers, a Monet pond with water lilies, and a few vaguely familiar others he couldn't name.

He examined a stack of clothes that included a down jacket, a couple of sweaters, and a scarf, finding nothing in any pockets or linings. Only a few pictures sat on the bottom shelf. One of Sarah and Vince together, one of Vince with his sons, and a couple of Sarah with two other women.

"Only two of those were from Vince," Sarah said. "But he had the other two framed for me."

Jay held the two pictures of her with the other women, one considerably older, one younger than Sarah. "Your mother and sister?"

She nodded. "I've already taken off the backs and looked to see if anything was hidden there. Nothing."

Clearly she didn't want him to do the same, so he set them down. He didn't see any way to fit a key in behind them.

An eclectic assortment of items remained on the shelf, mostly ornaments and knick-knacks. He picked up a graceful figurine of a tree branch with several birds perched on it and shook it gently. Nothing rattled. He looked at the bottom. A hole there showed it was hollow, but the opening wasn't wide enough to insert even a finger. Others were solid.

The only real possibility in that group was a porcelain music box that played a tune when the lid was raised. "Doesn't music have some kind of a key?" he asked, with vague memories of a school lesson in musical notation.

"A key signature. I'm not sure how that would help us. It's just a symbol you put on a piece of written music that shows where the scale begins. I don't see how it would be relevant. Of course, music boxes have keys too. The crank that you use to wind them up. Not that that's relevant either."

"But the connection might have occurred to Vince."

"True." She walked over to join him looking at the music box. The floral aroma of her perfume wafted around her, or maybe it was just the soap she used.

He turned the box over and released the catch to the compartment where the mechanism lay. The small space held nothing that shouldn't have been there. He closed it again and examined it from all sides but found no other obvious hiding place. A small wood trinket box was the only thing remaining on the shelf that might possibly hold a key, but a quick glance inside showed nothing.

He put it back. Sarah bit her lip to keep any disappointment from showing in her expression, but the very obvious effort told its own story.

"You know, it's just as possible Vince hid the key in something you already had. No reason he couldn't have gone into your room sometime while you weren't there."

"There's that." The tension in her cheeks eased.

"Take a careful look through everything as you unpack and place it. And let me know if you find anything at all. Anything you don't expect, even if it isn't obviously a key."

"I'll do it."

He left shortly thereafter. He had to get away before he gave in to the urge to pull her into his arms and kiss her senseless. He wanted her so badly, a fire burned in his veins and heated his muscles to the boiling point.

He got to work early and settled in to return phone calls and catch up on paperwork. Sam arrived an hour later. They compared notes on a few cases before they got to the Capelli murder.

"Anything?" Sam asked.

"Not a thing. You?"

"Just one thing. Capelli's neighbors aren't very close, but one on the other side of the street said she was awakened at a little after one the night of the murder by a noise she thought was firecrackers. A minute or so later, she heard the sound of a car door slamming and the screech of tires as a car left very quickly. She thought it came from Capelli's place. Not much, but it's another bit supporting the girl's story. Otherwise... I talked to Capelli's lawyer, the president of the bank he used, and all except for one person on the charity boards with him. They were all shocked, and no one admitted knowing he had any enemies so they couldn't speculate on who it might have been. More than one slyly suggested his live-in lover would bear some investigating."

"Did any of them have any concrete reason for it?"

"Nope. Just that she was there."

"Great."

The phone interrupted them. "Christianson?" Sergeant Graham's voice. "Need you and Hennesy in my office."

"In a minute." He put the phone back in its cradle. "Sergeant wants to see us."

"Any bets on what he wants?"

"Capelli. Hands down." Jay picked up his notes. He hated that they didn't have much to give on such a high profile case.

Sergeant Graham, the head of their unit, was actually pretty good as bosses went. He protected his people as much as possible and rarely made unreasonable demands. But he wasn't immune to pressure from above and sometimes could only do so much to deflect it.

This was one of those times.

"Tell me what you've got on the Capelli murder," he said when they were all seated.

Sam and Jay filled him on their investigation, what leads they'd pursued, and where they were now. Once they finished, the sergeant remained quiet for a few moments, staring at them.

"Why are you both so convinced this girl didn't do it? Everything points to her, including her fingerprints on the gun. It looks like a slam dunk. A few bruises don't make for a solid defense."

"There's also the blood trail out of the house," Jay said. "The shoe that made it doesn't match any in the house. But mostly it's the lack of motive. She had nothing to gain by Capelli's death and a lot to lose."

"She was there. She admits she held the gun. Heck, she even admits she fired it." The sergeant picked up a pen and began rolling it over and over in his fingers.

"While someone else held her hand on the gun. Reasonable doubt. Any decent defense attorney could plant it with what we've got. The bruises on her hand were consistent. Her story was consistent."

Sam continued the report with his own information. "The housekeeper says they hadn't argued, that in fact they seemed entirely normal that day. She swears Sarah Martin liked Vince. The girl is convincing. She's nice. She doesn't strike you as the kind of person it would take to set up a scenario like this. And a neighbor heard a car leave the Capelli place at the right time."

"Crap." The pen dropped and clattered against the desk. Graham picked it up again. "The chief wants some resolution on this. Something. Anything. He's getting a lot of heat on it. Capelli had friends in high places. We need to give them something soon."

"Any of that heat coming from sources we haven't looked at yet?" Jay asked.

"I'll get names from the captain," Graham promised.

"We're turning over every stone and pebble," Sam said. "We think the girl's the best bet for catching the killers since it looks like she has something they want."

"It would help if she had some idea what that was." The sergeant frowned.

"Actually we have a pretty good idea what it's likely to be," Jay said. "The thugs told the girl they were looking for the 'insurance.' And while there's plenty to suggest Capelli had some quasi-legal business, we didn't find any records of it. He told the girl she has the key. Too bad he didn't tell her where it was or when he'd given it to her."

"You've searched her stuff?"

"When we did the house. This afternoon I went over every gift she remembers Capelli giving her. Didn't find anything hidden."

The pen stilled. Graham flipped it, grabbed it by the point, and waved it at them. "We've got to get something soon or we're all in career limbo. Or worse. We could pull the girl in. Charge her with manslaughter or something."

Anger made Jay's gut churn. "Just so we can say we arrested *somebody*? The charges won't stick."

"It's marginal, but it might. Might buy us some breathing room, too."

"At her expense." Jay knew he shouldn't be showing so much outrage.

"She wants to catch the killer, too, doesn't she?"

"Yes. But she also wants to move on with her life. And it's less than clear to me how using her as a sacrificial goat would further the cause of justice."

"By buying us more time to work on it. And maybe, if the real killers think they're in the clear..." The sergeant rolled the pen between his fingers again.

Jay leaned forward. "They'll do what?"

"Try to find the key to the insurance while she's out of the way?"

There might be something to that, but Jay hated the thought of what it would do to Sarah. "Give us more time before we go to that."

"How much?"

"I don't know."

"It's not going to make me popular with the captain or the chief."

"You'll have the gratitude of your men."

Graham gave him a sour smile. "Like *that*'s going to count on my next review."

"We'll make you look good."

"Don't make promises you can't keep. I hope I'm not doing that now if I give you time. Just remember, I can't hold them off indefinitely." The sergeant stabbed the pen into his blotter. The new hole blended in with many others already there.

"We're not likely to forget," Sam said.

In the hallway, Sam said, "You'd better dial it back a notch, defending your girl. You covered it this time, but do it again and he's going to get suspicious."

"There's nothing to be suspicious of."

"Yeah, right. Tell me you're not affected by her at all."

Sam was just trying to keep him out of trouble, Jay reminded himself when anger surged through him. He unclenched his jaw. "We make judgments about people all the time. We like some, we don't like others. What's new about this?"

Sam shrugged. "I don't know if anything is. I'm just saying you'd better be watching your own reactions. You may be teetering on the verge of losing your impartiality."

Chapter 8

Sarah spent Sunday evening after Detective Christianson's visit trying not to think about him. She couldn't afford to indulge that nascent interest. Instead, she buried herself in writing the paper due the end of the week for her English Lit class. When not doing that, she worked on unpacking and organizing her things, checking out each item for some place Vince might have hidden a key.

Nothing turned up.

On Monday, she ran into Rob again after lunch, and he walked with her to her next class.

"The police made any progress figuring out who killed Vince?" he asked.

"Not that I know of."

"But they haven't arrested you yet."

"Obviously not."

"That's good."

They reached the building her class was in and she said goodbye to him.

"Sarah?"

She turned back to meet his earnest, concerned gaze.

"If you need help, let me know. I'd like to do what I can."

She smiled. "Thank you. I'll keep it in mind. I value your friendship very much."

Sarah went in to her class, hoping he'd gotten the message that friendship was all she wanted or could offer him.

She didn't see any cars following her home that evening. She did meet another set of neighbors, a young couple in one of the upstairs apartments. They were about the same age as she and had been married for a little over six months. She found them pleasant but wrapped up in themselves.

She made the acquaintance of another neighbor in a somewhat more traumatic way. On Tuesday afternoon, she got home from classes at three to find a note pinned to her door. It was from a neighbor upstairs she hadn't met, saying the woman had seen a burglar trying to break into Sarah's apartment that morning and had called the police.

As soon as she'd gone in and dropped her things, Sarah went upstairs and knocked on the door of 2H.

The woman who peered out of the partially opened door had a narrow face and deep lines around her eyes They introduced themselves and she let Sarah in.

"Got to be extra cautious," she said, "since I saw that burglar this morning. There he was, bold as brass, in daylight, trying to get in through one of your windows."

The woman wore a bathrobe and her hair stuck out in several directions. She stopped talking just long enough to get up and take care of a whistling tea kettle. Sarah declined the offer of a cup.

"I'm a nurse," the woman continued after she'd poured hot water into cup. "Work the night shift. Just got up, in fact. I usually hit the sack soon's I get home. Anyways, I got off at eight, same as always, this morning and came straight back here. I get up here about eight thirty and I hear this weird noise, like something scratching or scraping down below. I look out my window and there's this guy down on the ground, trying to open your window. He's got this weird mask over his face. So I call the cops, but wouldn't you know it, while I'm making the call, he looks up and sees me and runs away. Long gone by the time the cops got here."

"Why didn't someone try to call me?" she asked.

"Don't think anyone knew how to get in touch with you."

"Carlie, you there?" a voice called from downstairs. Sarah recognized Emily Petrie's voice. "Sarah back?" The older woman huffed her way up the stairs.

"I'm here," Sarah said. "Carlie told you about the burglar?"

"She did. I remembered your name but turns out there are a lot of Martins in the phone book."

"I'm not listed anyway. I just have a cell phone. Did you get the name of the police officer who investigated?" Sarah asked Carlie.

"I've got his card here. Just a moment." While she went to get it, the young couple in the next apartment arrived and stopped to see what the fuss was about. The group discussed security problems in the complex, other break-ins that had happened, a mugging or two, and how little the complex management did to address security problems, starting with their failure to replace burned-out light bulbs in the hall. They spent over an hour discussing the subject before they scattered.

Sarah called the police officer. He said he'd turned it over to a detective in the Burglary unit, who would be by her place shortly. She also called Christianson. He was on duty and promised to come as well.

She rejoined Mrs. Petrie and Carlie, who still talked at the top of the stairs.

"We ought to get together and discuss what we can do ourselves to help each other," Sarah said.

"We could do a pot luck supper sometime," Emily Petrie said. "It's a good idea to get to know each other and keep a watch out for each other."

They were interrupted in their attempts to work out a day and time by the arrival of Detective Christianson.

"Here comes your young man," Mrs. Petrie said to Sarah.

She wished. Oh how she wished. But… "He's not my young man. He's just a friend. He's also a police detective."

Christianson joined them. "What happened?" he asked. "Something about a burglary."

"Attempted," Sarah said. "Carlie can tell you."

While Carlie repeated the story, another woman arrived. The newcomer held up a badge as she approached but blinked in surprise when she saw Jay. "Christianson. I thought you were doing homicide these days."

"I am. Danielle? How're you doing? You're in Burglary now?"

"Yeah. They *called* it a promotion."

"From Vice, I wouldn't care what they called it as long as they called it out of there."

"Good point. Now tell me why you're here."

"I'll tell you in a bit. Let's go take a look at the scene." He turned to Carlie. "Will you show us where you saw the man?"

"Sure." She led the way down the stairs and around to the back of the building. They stopped at the corner.

Carlie, can you tell us exactly where you saw the burglar?" Jay asked. She pointed.

"Wait here, please." Jay held up a hand to stop them when they started to follow.

The two detectives examined the window the burglar had attempted to open. Sarah held Carlie's arm and stood in front of the others as they watched the police officers work. Danielle nodded to a couple of things and Christianson said a few words to her. They both looked particularly hard at one of the panes, but they didn't stay long before they came back.

Danielle focused on Sarah. "Miss Martin, can we go back to your place? I want to take a look from the inside, and I need to ask you a few questions."

"Of course." Sarah looked at her neighbor. "Let's plan for this weekend, if we can. We'll talk."

They agreed and dispersed, somewhat reluctantly. Sarah led both detectives into her apartment. "The window you were looking at is in my bedroom."

Again she followed them as they went to examine the site. Even she could see that the would-be burglar hadn't made much progress gaining entrance. What looked like a scratch on the glass, though, suggested an attempt at cutting through.

"There are lots of complications here," Christianson said to Danielle. "You heard about the Capelli murder?"

"Yeah. Two days' wonder in the papers. That one's yours? Wait--Sarah Martin. You're the girlfriend?"

Sarah nodded. Christianson explained to his colleague what had happened and who the likely burglar was.

"Nothing like keeping it simple," Danielle said.

"Sharing the misery," Christianson said. "Nothing about this case has been simple."

"Yeah." Danielle asked Sarah a few more questions about her schedule, whether it appeared anything had been taken, if she could think of any other reason for someone to try to break into her apartment. Once she had those answers, she left to write it up. "Keep me in the loop," she told Christianson.

Sarah expected him to leave too, but he didn't follow his colleague out right away.

Instead, he pointed to the bathroom. "What happened in there?"

The detritus from her failed efforts to hang a cabinet with shelves the previous evening still littered the room. She'd left a few tools sitting on the sink, and the shelf itself sat on the floor.

"Frustration. Lots of it. I bought this cabinet thing a couple of days ago and I was trying to put it up. There's no storage in the bathroom and not much anywhere else. But I don't know much about hanging things, and when I tried to screw in the screws I couldn't get them to go into the wall. I spent over an hour on it. I followed the directions and bought a stud finder and used that to find the best place to put the screws. They'd go in maybe half an inch, through the plaster if I hammered on them, but I couldn't get them into the wood at all."

His mouth curved in a wry one-sided grin. "You're supposed to drill a starter hole."

"It didn't say anything about that in the directions."

"I guess whoever wrote those assumed everyone knew that."

"And obviously that person didn't *know* everyone. I didn't know that. So I've got to go buy a drill now? What other tools do I need that I don't have?"

"I don't think you're ready to go drilling holes in your walls quite yet," he said, a note of humor lacing the words.

"You have a better idea?"

"Actually I do. What time do you get out of class tomorrow?"

"Wednesday? Three. I should be back here by three-thirty."

"Good. I'll bring a drill and an electric screwdriver."

"You'll what? I mean, thank you. But you don't have to do that. You don't owe me anything."

"It's not a debt. Just an attempt to help someone who needs it."

A flush heated her cheeks. "Oh, God, the last thing I want to be is someone's charity project."

"And the last thing I'm likely to do is take *on* a charity project. It's more like helping out a friend. Something I'd do for a neighbor if she needed it."

"Oh. Sorry to be so touchy. It's just kind of a sore subject. Thank you. Will you show me how to use them?"

"Power tools? Heck no. I may be a cop, but there are still some risks I'm not prepared to take."

"Then what's the point?"

"I'll do it."

"Oh. Would you mind then...helping me put up some curtain rods, too?"

His grin widened, though not enough to encompass his whole mouth. "Why not? Any other jobs?"

"I'll probably think of a couple more before you get here tomorrow."

"Okay, but remember. I don't rotate tires or change oil."

"No car maintenance. Got it."

He almost managed a full smile. Almost. Her heart almost skipped a beat and her face almost betrayed her feelings.

Christianson left.

Excitement created a full-force gale in her gut. If she could've done either competently, she'd be singing and dancing around the apartment.

Instead, Sarah forced herself to get to work on the paper due the end of the week and struggled to keep her mind on poets and poetry.

His face kept popping into her mind during classes the next day, too. Lean, steady jaw, nice cheekbones, and the light eyes that could be cold and menacing but could also shade warmer into concern and glow with humor.

Those memories made it even harder to be nice to Rob when he showed up to eat lunch with her again. She tried to keep him at arm's' length without actually cutting him off. The balancing act took more energy than she wanted to expend, but she didn't want to hurt him unnecessarily either. She suspected it would become necessary.

On the way home from campus that afternoon, though, something else distracted her, reminding her of the danger that still stalked her. A dark blue car. She couldn't remember seeing it as she pulled out of the student parking lot, but it was there when she made the first turn off the side road onto a more main one, and it stayed with her though two more turns that took her to the highway across town.

It remained a couple of car lengths back as she drove several miles to her exit, changing lanes when she did, and it followed her down the ramp off the highway. When she turned into the parking lot of her apartment, the other car went by, but a motor sounded and tires crunched at the far end. A building blocked her view, so she couldn't see if it was the same one that had followed her. She waited inside the car with the doors locked for a few minutes. No other vehicles pulled up closer and she didn't see anyone around.

Still, she held her breath when she got out until she made it into the apartment and locked the door behind her.

When the doorbell buzzed, she looked through the peephole twice before opening it to Christianson.

Something must have shown on her face, though.

"What happened?" he asked, setting down a large metal toolbox.

She told him about the car she thought was following.

"I don't suppose you got a license plate number?"

"It was behind me."

"If it happens again, try to find a way to get behind it. See if you can circle around. Or pull to the side of the road and let it go by. An ID on the car could be a big break in helping us solve this."

"All right. I will."

"Good. Now…" He bent down to unlatch the box. "What first?"

"Curtain rods, I think."

"Okay."

She handed him the hardware and showed him where she wanted it.

"I see you've mastered a hammer and nails." He glanced at the pictures she'd hung the previous night during a break from writing about themes of love and loss in poetry. The cheaply framed prints of flower paintings brightened up the room, making the dingy off-white paint less noticeable.

"I don't know if I'd call it mastery," she said. "More like we've reached a working relationship. I don't try to drive the nail in too far and the hammer only mashes my fingers once or twice a picture."

"Only once or twice? You're doing well."

He took an electric drill from the toolbox and plugged it in. She couldn't help staring at him as he bent to do it. The jeans and Henley shirt hugged his long body, highlighting wide shoulders that tapered to a lean waist and hips. The butterflies danced in her stomach. "Show me where to put it," he said.

Though he was almost six-two, Christianson still had to stand on her desk chair to reach above the windows. Sarah helped him get the rods level, held nails and screws, and passed him tools. He accomplished in twenty minutes what would have taken her hours.

Then they tackled the bathroom shelf she'd tried to install herself. That was where things got more difficult.

The room was small and the space over the john where she wanted to hang the shelf cabinet, tight.

"Show me about how high you want it," Christianson said, holding up the shelf.

"A little lower."

He slid it down.

"That's good," Sarah said.

"Come hold this while I get it level and mark the spot."

She had to wiggle past him and slide under his arms to reach the shelf. It put her back against the length of his body. The tight space forced them together, making her too vividly aware of his warmth and scent, the hardness of his chest, and his masculine reaction to a woman's bottom pressed against his hips. Heat bubbled in her blood and made all her nerve endings sing.

He placed the level on top. He had to put his hands over hers to slide the thing up and down until he had it positioned properly. He made quick pencil marks to guide him in drilling the holes. "Okay, got it," he said.

She slid away, hoping the heat she felt didn't mean her face was as flaming red as she feared.

"Get me a ruler, please." He studied the marks he'd made on the wall and the position of the hangers on the back of the shelf with more concentration than the job warranted until she left the room.

When Sarah returned, he measured the back of the shelf and then down the wall from his marks. He drilled holes and used an electric screwdriver to start the screws before he backed them out again.

"This is where it gets tricky," he said. "I need you to hold this very steady for me."

Sarah moved in closer to take the weight of the shelf and hold it. Keeping it still proved a challenge. Her hands wanted to tremble. Her entire body vibrated in response to being close to him. She couldn't be sure, but she thought she felt a bit of a quiver from him. If so, he didn't acknowledge it. He had to bend awkwardly to position the screws in the holes, pushing his elbow into her breast.

"Sorry," he said.

"Not to worry." *That shouldn't feel so good.* "I appreciate your doing this. I never would have gotten this thing installed myself."

"Give you a course or two at Home Depot and a couple of months of practice and you might have."

He finally got the first screw positioned and used the electric screwdriver to drive it in. She fought the shelf's tendency to rotate with the screw, holding it tightly in place.

He leaned back. "One down, two to go."

She moved to accommodate his repositioning for the second screw. He stood beside her. Their hips pressed together and even their shoulders touched due to the awkward bend he had to make to get to the screw hole.

Electric sparks radiated from every place their bodies came together. She had to keep her mind on hanging shelves. Had to. Couldn't afford to think about the man so close. The man she wanted to get even closer to. The man she wanted to touch and feel and… Damn it. Concentrate on the keeping the shelf steady. It tried to buck when he tightened the screw.

"Hold it," he said as the thing jolted.

"Trying, Detective."

"Jay," he said.

"What?"

"Call me Jay. Everyone else does."

She clenched her teeth and tightened her grip on the shelf. And on herself. She was not a hormone-driven teenager. She should be more mature. Have better control. "Is that your real name?"

"No." He swore as the screwdriver jumped off the head of the screw. "Sorry about that. It's Jeremiah Thomas. I've always gone by my initials, J.T., so my brothers just started calling me Jay."

"Wow. Jeremiah Thomas is a mouthful."

"You're not kidding. Not sure what my parents were thinking. Especially when my brothers got normal names like Andrew and William. There." He backed away. "Two down. One left. Change places with me. This shouldn't be as hard. The other two screws will mostly hold it."

She nodded. Arms and thighs brushed as they shifted positions. They had to adjust when he tried to insert the screw and his elbow ended up resting on her breast again.

Her nipple puckered. Heat poured through her, making her blood fizz and her head light. Tension drew up her muscles tight, though she could pretend it was just the effort of holding the shelf in place. How much longer could she bear this position?

"There. That's got it." He backed away, giving her a bit of breathing room.

Because she couldn't look at him at the moment, she turned her attention to the shelf. "Fantastic!" she said. "You did a great job." He had, too. The shelf hung exactly where she wanted it, level and perfect. "I can't tell you how much this helps me."

She swiveled toward him and caught an odd look on his face: intent, rapt, almost hungry. He stared at her like she was a banquet he longed for and couldn't get near.

"It's okay," he said, stumbling back a step, out of the bathroom. He stopped in the hall.

She followed him, but when she would have gone by, he put a hand on her arm.

"Sarah?"

She halted and looked up. He still wore that steady, serious, hungry expression. Something about it drilled its way inside her, curling down through her chest, into her heart and spreading lower. His gaze resting on her face felt almost physical, hot and heavy, as it roused an answering longing inside her.

He dipped his head toward her and his mouth lowered onto hers. It started light and gentle, a soft, smooth glide of his lips over hers, until sparks ignited where their mouths joined. Little snaps of electricity jolted through her. Every part of her heated, softened, and tried to melt against him. His muscles clenched tighter and harder. The arm that went around her shoulders was so taut it shook. Or maybe she was doing the shaking. When his tongue nudged at her lips, she opened and let him in.

He filled her senses with his distinctive male aroma mixed with some piney fragrance, the rough knit of his shirt over the hard muscles of his back, and the length of his body moving in close to hers. More than anything else though, the exquisite brush of his tongue over her mouth sent sparkles of pleasure rushing through her. She opened her mouth and let him in. His tongue tangled with hers, swiped her gums, explored the sensitive surfaces. Pressure roared in her head. Blood rushed through her veins and a heaviness gathered between her legs. She closed her eyes, surrendering. Every nerve-end in her body fired. Tingles ran along her skin, running up and down all the way to her toes.

The man knew how to kiss.

She couldn't think of anything but the feel of his mouth on hers, the way they meshed and blended into each other. She almost lost herself. Nothing had ever bowled her over as this had. Vince had done it, but it had never turned her on like this. Although she'd liked him, Vince had never made every nerve in her body sing with desire and need. He'd never brought her to the verge of going up in flame.

Jay's kiss combined a deep tenderness with raw, fiery longing. It danced through every corner of her being, arousing parts of her body and soul no man had ever touched before.

She sank into it, wanting to lose herself, drowning and not caring at all.

He rubbed her back, fingers massaging the tight muscles, before trailing down to cup her buttocks and lift her toward him. She pressed closer, wanting to feel every inch of him. She reached for the hem of his shirt.

A loud buzzing from the vicinity of his waist startled them both into jumping apart. Until he reached down, pulled it out, and flipped it open, she didn't realize it was his cell phone.

Sarah struggled to get her breathing back under control and quiet the raging demands of her body as she listened to him say hello and promise he wouldn't forget some errand he was supposed to do. From his tone and the way he laughed, she deduced it wasn't a business call.

Though nothing in his voice indicated how much the kiss had affected him, the hand that held the cell phone still trembled.

He looked at her. "I don't know. I'll ask. I guess so." After a brief goodbye he snapped the phone closed.

"My sister-in-law says she's got a small table with a couple of chairs sitting in the attic and wondered if you could use them. She says they're not beautiful or in the greatest of shape, but not terrible either. They're taking up space she needs and if you don't want them, she's giving them to the Salvation Army." He shrugged. "She's embarrassed about offering you hand-me-downs, but says it would be a favor if you'd take them off her hands and get them out of the way. If you want them, Will can drop them off here on Saturday."

She struggled to collect her scattered senses and make sense of his words. Part of her wanted to rush back into his arms and demand they finish what they'd started. But while he talked on the phone, her brain had regained control over the raging desire. "I suppose... Sure, why not? I need a table and chairs. If it helps her find more room, that's a bonus, I guess."

"Good. I'll let her know." The glittering lights no longer shone in his blue eyes. Shadows had returned. He had his expression under tight control again, leaving nothing to read in his face except that he didn't intend to kiss her again.

"Sarah, I'm--"

"Don't. Please. It was a kiss. It was nice. It didn't mean anything." *Keep it light. He doesn't need to know about all the frustration of unfulfilled desire and lost closeness.*

He stared at her and his face tightened. "The hell it didn't. But that's the problem. It can't be anything more. Not right now. Maybe never."

"Because I'm still a suspect in Vince's murder."

Jay nodded.

"And you might have to arrest me for it yet." She hoped he'd deny it and reassure her it wasn't likely.

"It's possible."

She'd more or less expected it, but the words still felt like a punch to the gut. She struggled to keep the reaction from showing.

"I was going to offer to take you out to dinner or something," she said. "To thank you. You've been a lot more helpful than I had any right to expect. But I guess it probably isn't a good idea."

"It isn't a good idea. There's no reason why you should feel obliged to buy me anything."

"Not an obligation. Just a desire. Forget I mentioned it. Please."

"No."

"Jay--"

"I don't want to forget you offered. Sarah." He leaned over and put a gentle finger on her lips. "This isn't easy for you. It isn't for me either. If things were different--"

"If I weren't a murder suspect."

"If you weren't a murder suspect, I'd be asking you for a date. And doing a lot more than just kissing." His mouth crooked into the half-grin. "Or trying to, anyway. But as it is, I can't. I just can't. Which isn't to say I'm not tempted. Sarah, I'm so damned tempted, but…"

She nodded. "I understand. Your job's important to you. And your integrity, maybe even more so. I admire that. It's part of what attracts me about you." She didn't want to understand. She wanted to rage and scream at the injustice and beg him to ignore everything but the fire between them.

"You're just *not* going to make this any easier, are you?" The surface amusement didn't quite hide the pain and longing in his voice.

"I'm trying to."

"I know. That's the hell of it. You do understand. And you're trying to act on it. It makes you… Oh, hell." He sighed heavily.

"Detec-- Jay, do you really believe I--? No, forget I asked. Please. It doesn't really matter."

His lips tightened. "You're right that it might not matter, but not in the way you think. It might not matter what I think about the case at all. There's a lot of pressure coming down to make an arrest."

"And I'm still the person most likely to be arrested."

He nodded.

"What happens if you never figure out who did it?"

"Most likely we'll end up arresting you."

Sarah heaved in a deep breath and then struggled to keep it from sounding like a sob as she released it. "I'll go to trial for murder. Will I be convicted?"

"Probably not, if you get a good lawyer."

"Well, that's some relief. Of course, there is that 'probably' in there. Still, I'd have to pay a small fortune for a lawyer, which would use up everything I've saved for my education, plus I'd lose a lot of time, and I'd have an arrest on my record."

He looked away from her. "There's also a possibility you could be convicted of a lesser charge."

"Okay. I get it. I'd damn well better hope you figure out who really did this. Hope, no! I need to *do* everything I can to help or my future isn't worth the price of a cup of coffee. As for us… It's better we don't push anything. Can I at least say thank you? You've gone well beyond the call of duty to help me and I do appreciate it."

"Sarah, you need to be careful. The best thing you can do is try to figure out where the key Vince gave you is and what it is. And maybe get a license number for the people following you, if you can do it without attracting their attention."

"I'm certainly going to do that. But Jay… I may have to do more. My future is at stake. Maybe my life. And what, exactly, is safety? In my position, sitting around doing nothing could be a lot riskier than trying to find out who did want Vince dead."

He sighed, leaned forward, and kissed her forehead. "I'd better get going. I understand why you want to do more, but I still want you to be careful. Whoever wanted Vince dead is ruthless and clever. He's more than willing to let you be the patsy, but if you show signs of getting closer, he'd probably be just as happy to have you dead, too."

Chapter 9

The next day, Sarah made an effort to be alert and careful when she left for classes and again when she returned. But she saw no vehicle following and no one accosted her. She couldn't help being disappointed. She'd given them every opportunity. She didn't see Rob that day and gave thanks for small blessings. She liked him, but he was becoming another problem in a life already too full of them.

After her last class ended she called Marc. He was tied up in meetings but offered to meet her for lunch the next day, Friday.

Following an idea that occurred to her in class that morning, when she got home on Thursday, she went through every piece of clothing she owned, checking pockets and linings with particular care.

Unfortunately she found nothing but a couple of old gas receipts, a ticket stub from a movie theater, a lipstick she'd assumed lost some time ago, and a lot of lint.

Later that evening, around seven, a commotion outside the apartment caught her attention. A quick scan through the peephole showed nothing, so she opened the door a crack and peered out, hoping it wasn't a distraction intended to lure her into an ambush. But when she leaned into the hall, lights from a police vehicle flashed in the parking lot and most of the other residents of the block had gathered in front of the building.

She locked up and stuffed the key in the pocket of her jeans before she went out to join them.

One police officer shone his flashlight around the walk, while the other talked to the neighbor she'd met when she'd first moved in. Sarah fished her name out of memory. Pam. If she'd heard a last name she couldn't remember it.

Carlie and Emily Petrie huddled together near the building's entrance. She approached them. "What happened?"

"Pam got mugged," Emily said. "Right there on the walk. Someone tried to grab her."

"Good lord. She looks okay. I take it she wasn't hurt? Did they try to grab her purse?"

"Not sure," Carlie said. "Doesn't look like she's hurt. I think I heard her tell the cop one of them grabbed her arm and swung her around."

"She said they asked her something like 'You got anything?' Does that make any sense?" Emily said. "Unless she was dealing drugs or something. But I can't see our Pam doing that. Some other things, yes, but not drugs. Of course, maybe…"

"She doesn't," Carlie said. "I've seen enough of it at the hospital. I'd recognize it."

"Did she know them?" Sarah asked.

"Don't think so," Emily said. "I think she said they were wearing masks."

Suspicion roused in Sarah. "Like the mask the guy who tried to break into my apartment was wearing? And he wanted something from her?"

Emily looked confused but Carlie focused a hard stare at her. "You think they mistook her for you?"

Sarah stared at Pam. The woman wore a dark gray hooded sweatshirt over her jeans. Sarah didn't own anything like that, but they wouldn't know. And she and Pam both stood about five-foot-six. "If she had the hood up, it's possible. And it's cool enough, she might have put it up." Sarah had begun to shiver, too, but something more than just the chill in the air caused it.

"What's going on with you?" Carlie asked.

"Later. I'll tell you later," Sarah promised.

The police officer who'd been interviewing Pam approached them. "I understand you all live in the building." He asked a series of questions about where they'd been that evening, if they'd seen anyone in the area acting suspiciously, and other crimes in the area they knew of.

Carlie and Sarah both mentioned the attempt to break into her apartment. The officer questioned them at some length about it, and his interest piqued when they told him about the mask worn by the would-be burglar.

When he slowed down, Sarah asked if she could talk to him privately. He frowned, shrugged, and nodded for her to follow him away from the others.

"What can I do for you?" he asked.

"Actually I wanted to tell you what probably happened." She went on to identify herself and explain who she thought the would-be muggers were and why they'd accosted Pam.

"So you think these men mistook her for you?"

"You can check the case record for the Capelli murder," she said. "Men wearing ski masks forced their way into my apartment last week and said they wanted something from me. They threatened me and said that I'd better find it for them."

The officer studied her face for a moment. "Okay. It's possible. I'll make a note of it. You need to be careful, if you really think these guys were after you."

"I know," she said. "And I am."

He finished up more paperwork and departed. It was after nine by then. She still had to finish proofing her paper, but she also wanted to talk to Pam, so she hung around waiting. Several of the other neighbors wanted to hear her story too. Pam invited them all to come back to her place. Carlie retrieved a bottle of wine from her apartment to share.

Pam's story was pretty simple. She arrived home from work just before dark. As she walked from her car to the building, two men raced out from around a corner of the apartment block and grabbed her. One put an arm around her throat; the other clutched her elbow.

The man holding her by the throat growled, "Have you found it yet? Don't think you can give it to the cops or someone else."

"I told them I didn't know what they were talking about. I think that's when they realized they'd made a mistake and I wasn't the person they wanted. The one holding me sort of tossed me aside then, and they took off. That was all. It rattled me. I guess I'm pretty lucky they didn't actually hurt me or take anything."

"You are," Sarah said. "But I have to ask. Did you have the hood up, so they couldn't see your face?"

Pam's eyebrows rose. "Yeah, I did. It's chilly."

"That's probably why they mistook you for someone else."

"I'll never wear a hood up again," Pam vowed.

"It'll probably never happen again."

"These guys sound similar to the one Carlie said tried to break into your apartment."

Sarah looked around at her gathered neighbors. She really didn't want to admit this, but she owed it to them. "I'm guessing they were the same ones."

"And they mistook me for you?" Pam said. "We're about the same height and build."

"Most likely."

"So what's the story?" Carlie asked. "What do those men want?"

"I wish I knew," Sarah said. "I'd be a lot better off if I did." She wrapped her arms around herself. It was still chilly in the apartment and she had goose bumps on her arms. "Do you remember reading in the paper a few weeks ago about the murder of a man named Vince Capelli?"

Most of the people in the room looked blank, but Emily Petrie said, "I remember. Wasn't he that mobster that was killed by his mistress?"

She shivered. "He wasn't a mobster, though he might have been involved in some illegal business ventures. And his mistress didn't kill him. At least, I didn't want to or try to." She went on to tell them most of the story.

When she finished, everyone stared at her wide-eyed. She waited for them to say something. Despite the cool air, sweat started on her temples and crept down under her shirt. She felt like she was on trial and awaiting a verdict. Was this a foretaste of what that would be like?

"I never would've guessed you'd been involved in something like that," Carlie said.

Sarah tried to dissect her tone, searching for condemnation.

"That must have been horrible for you." Emily handed her a sweater. Sarah would've felt guilty about accepting it, but the woman already wore two others.

An older man named Rick, who lived upstairs, added, "They haven't figured out who those men are yet, have they? You think the guys who tried to grab Pam tonight are the same ones who forced you to shoot?"

"Yes, I think so."

"Makes them pretty dangerous, then," he said.

"Very dangerous."

"We got to keep close watch on what's going on around here." Rick swept an arm around to encompass the entire complex. "Keep an eye out for those guys. If anybody sees hide or hair of them we call the police and call each other. Make sure the others who live in the building but ain't here with us now know about this, too. Maybe in some of the other buildings around. We can spread the word."

"We see them, we'll tackle them and capture them for you," Emily said.

"You'll beat them with your cane?" Sarcasm edged the words Rick directed at Emily.

"You going to cut them with the sharp edge of your tongue?" she shot back. "That's all you got left that's still sharp."

"How would you know?" he asked. "You can't see worth a damn and you can hardly move."

Emily sidled over and poked him in the chest with a finger. "My body may be giving out, but my brain's still working. More than you can say."

"You don't have brains enough to go to the doctor when you need to. I don't see how you--"

"Emily, Rick." Carlie raised her voice, cutting across the exchange. "We don't need this. We need to be working together not bickering."

"And nobody's tackling anybody," Sarah added. "That's for the police to do. I don't want to be responsible for anyone getting hurt trying to help me. All you need to do is watch and call the police if you see any suspicious characters around. Especially if they happen to be wearing a ski mask."

"We need to talk to management about getting the outside lights replaced faster," Carlie said. "Half the bulbs are out right now, including two of them in the breezeway. I called them last week to tell them about it, and nothing's been done yet. Maybe we could talk to the police and get someone to check around here regularly too."

"I'd be willing to make a couple of phone calls," the female half of the couple in 2E said. "I'll see if I can set up a time for us to meet with the complex manager. It would be good if as many as possible of us could go."

They spent another half hour or so making plans, including a potluck supper on Sunday evening, and then they scattered to their own apartments. Since Emily was at the back of the hall opposite her, she and Sarah separated from the others. Sarah had to slow her pace so the older woman could keep up. Emily hobbled stiffly.

"Was Rick right that you need to go to the doctor?" Sarah asked. "Why don't you?"

The woman shrugged. "It's just too much trouble. I don't drive and a cab's too expensive, so I either got to wait for a bus or get that service for the elderly. I have a hard time with both of them."

Sarah debated. She didn't have a lot of extra time and might be inviting more danger to herself. But she'd just been talking with her neighbors about helping each other, and they'd jumped in to support her. "I could drive you, if we can set up an appointment time when I don't have classes."

"Oh, no, hon, I couldn't ask you to do that. You're a busy young woman between college and your young man."

"I could find the time. How about I come over tomorrow afternoon and we can call and make the appointment?"

"Well, if you really think you have the time, I suppose we should."

"I'm sure you should. I'll see you tomorrow."

Sarah handed the sweater back, and then went back inside her apartment, careful to lock the door, throw the deadbolt, and fasten the chain behind her. She pulled out her cell phone to call Christianson but paused when she saw the time displayed. Ten forty. She didn't know if he was on duty that evening, but if not, she didn't want to disturb him at such a late hour.

In truth, she wanted to disturb him, she just didn't think she should. The sound of his voice could make her heartbeat speed up and curls of joy unwind in her chest. She wanted him nearby. He made her feel safe. It was an illusion, of course. He represented another sort of danger to her, possibly in more ways than one.

Strange though, that she was simply happier when he was around.

She was falling in love with him, probably the worst thing she could do under the circumstances.

But something deep inside her, something that connected with Jay Christianson on the physical level and several deeper ones, didn't care about the circumstances.

He admitted some attraction on his side, too, and that didn't help at all. She fell asleep that evening, picturing his face. The lean cheeks and jaw, prominent cheekbones, bright light blue eyes, and the delicious creases that bracketed his mouth when he smiled the rare smile--all soothed her somehow.

She got up early to print off a final copy of the paper to turn in and proceeded carefully as she walked out to her car, got in, and headed to the campus. No one jumped out at her, nor did any vehicles follow her on the road.

Later that day, as she drove a couple of miles to the restaurant to meet Marc for lunch, she kept watch again, but still nothing happened. Frustrating. Just as she figured out they offered her a possible chance to prove her innocence, her pursuers disappeared.

Marc arrived a few minutes after she did. He asked how she was doing in her new apartment and how her classes were going. Conversation stayed on safe topics until after they'd ordered their meals and the server had departed.

Then he asked, "What's up? Have they made any progress in figuring out who killed Dad? No one will tell me a damn thing."

"You're not alone. The police aren't really into sharing what they know with civilians. But the detective, Christianson, did say they don't have any good suspects right now--other than me."

"I hear an 'and' appended to that. You're either doing something about it now or planning to do something. I suppose that's why you wanted to talk to me?"

Sympathy, impatience, and disapproval mingled in Marc's expression. It made his handsome face very appealing, but in a friends-only sort of way. He hadn't been close to his father. In fact, they'd argued quite a bit, though they tended to do so behind closed doors. She'd wondered occasionally about the subject of their arguments. Marc might not approve of his father's less legal or at least more ethically questionable ventures.

"Look at it this way. If they don't catch whoever did it, at best I'm going to spend the rest of my life with the shadow of this hanging over me. At worst, I could go on trial for murder. Detective Christianson admitted he was getting pressure to make an arrest. Who's that likely to be?"

His lips twisted into a frown. "I understand that, but still, it's got to be dangerous to pursue it any further. They killed my dad."

"Don't you want to know who did it?"

"Hell, yes, but not at the expense of someone else's safety. I'm rooting for the cops to solve this one. Those detectives struck me as pretty good at their job, even if the younger one was looking a bit moonstruck whenever he turned your way."

"He's not so moonstruck he won't arrest me if he has to."

"If it ever comes to that, let me know. I'll bail you out and get you a really good lawyer."

"I appreciate it. I hope I don't have to take you up on that offer, which is why I need to ask a couple of questions. I don't know anything at all about your dad's business... The above-board part and the not-so-above-board part."

"He didn't discuss it much with anyone, except the people he did business with," Marc said. "He didn't even tell us much about it. Dan probably knows more than I do, but not by much."

Sarah picked up her water glass and took a sip. "What about in his papers? Didn't you go through those?"

"We did. It was pretty much all stuff about his investments. He had a lot of them. And he did consulting on currency exchanges, particularly from some of the smaller less-developed countries. As far as I could tell, all of those were legal, legitimate businesses."

"But he had some that weren't. He may have made the bulk of his money on them."

Marc shrugged and waited while the server delivered their meals. "I'm pretty sure he did too. But there were only a few things in his records to suggest it. Some of the deposits and tax records. Not enough to track down what he was doing or who he was doing it with."

"What about his phone book? And did you check the speed dials on his cell phone?"

"The police still have his little pocket phone list. And his cell phone was smashed when he...was killed. I don't know if the police recovered any information from it."

Sarah had started to fork up a bite of manicotti but put it down again. "If Christianson is telling the truth and they don't have many leads, I'm guessing not. But it doesn't make sense. How could he do business daily and not keep any notes about it, any records...anything?"

Marc raised his eyebrows. "That's a good point. Unless everything was done through someone else? So he only had to keep one number in his head."

"But surely the police have looked at his phone records. If he called someone that often, they would have noticed."

Marc shrugged. "I suppose so. I'm just throwing out ideas. Maybe it was the kind of business that didn't need a lot of intervention on his part. Like maybe he just funded something...somehow."

"Could be." Depression crept over her.

Marc paused in the middle of wiping his mouth with a napkin. "What's the matter?"

"It's just... I feel like I'm in a vise and it's closing in on me. If I don't get some kind of lead, something the police can pursue--something or someone other than me--they're going to arrest me. And there doesn't seem to be much I can do about it."

"Maybe you should think about getting a lawyer now."

"I thought about it, but I hate to spend the money unless I have to. I don't have all that much and I want to make it last as long as I can. But maybe... Can you recommend one?"

Marc nodded as he took a bite of roll. "He doesn't come cheap, though."

"Can you give me his name, so if I do need one I'll know who to call?"

He set down the bread and pulled a pen and one of his business cards from his packet. On the back of the card he wrote a name and phone number. "He only takes a limited number of clients. Tell him I referred you. That'll get you in the door."

"I will. Thanks."

He gave a harsh laugh. "I know it isn't the kind of help you'd hoped for from me."

She shrugged. "I'm taking stabs in the dark. Flailing around trying to get hold of something, anything that could help. I didn't really expect anything. Shoot. The police haven't come up with anything yet, why should I be able to?"

"Because you knew Dad better. And he did trust you with 'the key.' Whatever that means."

"Too bad he wasn't a bit more specific about what it was. And where. Fat lot of good it's doing anyone when I can't find it."

Marc started to pick up a glass of water but set it down again without taking a sip. "You've searched?"

"Just everything I own. More than once. Believe me. Since it's my only real lead, I've racked my brain and examined everything I own. I don't have very much so it wasn't too hard. Nothing. I just have no clue what he meant."

"What about the furniture?"

"There weren't any keys taped to the bottom of my bookshelves or the desk. No hidden drawers or compartments. I've gone over everything more than once. So has Christianson. Neither of us found anything. I don't know about the other furniture that was in my room. I have to think the cops must have checked it, too."

"Most likely."

"Do you have any ideas? Does the idea of a key rouse any memories or connections for you?"

"I've done plenty of racking my brain, too," he said. "If I had any ideas you'd have heard about them."

They spent the rest of the meal going through their associations with the word "key" but nothing brought any useful ideas or recalled anything significant for either of them.

Marc insisted on paying, over Sarah's objections, but in the end she let him. He could afford it more easily than she could. She had one more class that afternoon. She struggled to keep her attention focused on conjugating French verbs when so many other things pressed on her.

After dropping her bag and picking up the mail at home, she went across the hall and knocked on Emily Petrie's door. A couple of minutes passed before the woman answered.

"I came to see if we could set up an appointment with your doctor," Sarah said.

"Oh, right. Have a seat and let me go find the number."

Sarah looked around the cluttered space and finally pushed aside a stack of magazines on a chair to make space to sit. Emily puttered around for several minutes in the bedroom. She came back and scrabbled around in a desk in the living room before she finally extracted a little booklet.

"Here it is." She toddled across the room to the little table where her phone sat, picked up the receiver, and dialed slowly. It took a few minutes to get through and explain who she was, but apparently the people on the other end very much wanted to see her. Quickly.

"Monday?" the woman said. "I don't know. Hold on. Let me ask." She turned to Sarah. "Could you take me on Monday?"

"If it's after three."

The woman relayed that to the person on the other end and they settled on an appointment at four. Sarah got the name and address of the place and said goodbye to the woman, promising to see her later.

She spent the evening catching up on chores and doing some basic cleaning, trying not to think too much about Detective Jay Christianson. He'd said his brother would stop by the next day to drop off a table and chairs. She didn't want to hope he'd come too.

Jay called at nine thirty the next morning. "I've got my brother's truck and we're loading the table and chairs on it now. I should be there in half an hour. Is that okay with you?"

Stay cool. "Yes. Fine." Her voice didn't shake too noticeably on the words.

"Good. Be there shortly."

Calm. She had to be calm. But the butterflies in her stomach were turning somersaults.

Forty minutes later he knocked at her door. Her heart skipped and began pounding harder when she peered through the peephole and saw him. Damn, she was acting like a teenager with a crush.

He smiled when she opened the door. A nearly full smile, showing off the creases in his cheeks and putting glittering sparks in his light blue eyes. Muscles in her chest twisted, rousing a combination of pleasure and pain.

"Sorry it took longer than I planned," he said, "but I bet you won't mind when you hear why. Anyway, I'll go get the stuff from the truck. It'll take more than one trip."

"I'll help." She snagged a jacket from the closet and followed him out to the truck. The weather had turned chillier overnight, the first real cold snap of Fall, not too surprising for late October. While walking behind him, she admired the athletic grace of his long stride, the way the leather bomber jacket emphasized his broad shoulders and the worn jeans clung to long, lean legs. The cool breeze ruffled his dark hair.

The table sitting in the back of the pickup was in better condition than he'd led her to believe. Not a classy or obviously expensive piece of furniture, but it hadn't come from a cheapo-mart either, and it had been gently used. A stack of chairs lay beside it.

"Looks almost like new," she said, helping him lift a chair out. "Are you sure they were just giving this away?"

He shrugged and hopped up onto the bed of the truck to slide the table to the end. "Lisa said she wanted it gone. They redid their kitchen, and it doesn't go with the new set-up or something. Anyway they've got three kids now, so they needed something bigger."

"Your brother has three kids?"

"Yeah. And he's only two years older than me. Got a big head start. On the other hand, I notice he's already got some gray hairs."

She stopped and stared at him. The sunlight shone on a few silvery strands in his hair as he climbed down again. "You do too."

"It's my job. Ages people before their time. And he has more. Help me get this down."

Together they carried the table into her apartment and then went back for the chairs.

"I've got a few more things out there," he said as he placed the last chair beside the table. "That was what took me so long. I passed a yard sale on the way and saw some things I thought you could use, so I stopped." They went back out and he climbed up into the truck again.

The lump in her throat made it hard to talk. "That was thoughtful of you."

"No problem." He slid a microwave oven toward her. "The guy I bought it from swears it works. I haven't lost much if it doesn't." Jay pushed a box in her direction. "You won't believe how much these cost." The carton held a complete eight-piece service of dishes, a set of drinking glasses, and cutlery. "Five bucks for the whole thing. Take what you need and dump the rest."

"Great. I do need these." She took the box into the apartment.

Jay followed her with the microwave. She made room for it on the counter and he plugged it in. He took a cup from the box, filled it with water, and stuck it in the microwave. The machine began to hum. When it buzzed a minute later, the water in the cup was hot.

"Looks like it works. Good. I've got one more thing to bring in. Wait here. I can get this myself."

"Okay." Sarah unloaded dishes from the box and put them in the sink to wash before she used them.

Jay returned minutes later carrying a framed painting about four feet wide and eighteen inches tall. When he turned it around, she saw a landscape showing a series of rolling hills in the background. A meadow comprised most of the foreground, dominated by a field of flowers, yellow buttercups and bright blue chicory.

Her heart did a strange little jump. For a few moments she could only stare at it, entranced. "It's beautiful. Perfect. It's for me?"

"The moment I saw it, I knew it was for you." He stood it in front of the worn recliner Pam had given her. "Let me get the tools from the truck and we can hang it." He paused. "If you want it."

"Of course, I want it. Yes, please, I want it right there." She pointed to the expanse of blank wall that faced the door.

Jay returned in a moment with a metal toolbox. Though she helped him get the picture positioned properly, they didn't have the same issues as they'd had hanging the shelf in the bathroom since space wasn't as tight and she didn't have to hold the picture once he'd marked the position for the hanger.

It didn't take him long, either.

The picture transformed the room, turning it from drab with spotty attempts to brighten it into a place dominated by the brilliant, ebullient meadow. It certainly didn't qualify as great art. Experts would likely label it pedestrian at best. But it touched her. It had a sunny, optimistic purity that made her smile. And Jay had bought it for her. That made her smile inside.

"It looks wonderful there," she said. "And it lights up the entire room. Thank you so much. And please thank your brother and sister-in-law for the table and chairs. You and your family have been very generous."

He pushed dark hair back from his forehead. "You want to repay me? I have a lonely Saturday ahead. Let's do something interesting. There are a couple of museums I've been meaning to visit, but somehow never get around to it. You up?"

"It sounds like fun. Will you let me buy you lunch? I owe you at least that."

He studied her with a frown and narrowed eyes but after a moment he relented. "All right. You're on."

They had a wonderful day, though little about what they did was spectacular or memorable. What lingered in Sarah's memory was how much she enjoyed being with Jay, how easy it was to talk to him, the way they laughed at the same things, how they could kid and tease each other and occasionally touch each other, letting the sparks of desire fly, unfulfilled, and still enjoy the experience. By the end of the day, when Jay brought her home, she no longer suspected she was falling in love with him. She knew it. Or rather she knew she'd fallen. Deeply, thoroughly, irrevocably. It would likely lead to heartbreak and pain, but she could at least tell herself she knew what it felt like to be in love.

She invited him in when he escorted her to the door of her apartment, but he declined. Before he left though, he pulled her close. For a few moments, he held her against him with her head resting on his shoulder. His solid form offered shelter and protection. The scent of leather and a piney fragrance he wore teased her with the promise of…not just his masculine essence, but the deeper essence of a man who would be there, who would stand firmly with anyone he cared about. Warmth, contentment, and peace added up to a quiet joy.

Then he moved and she straightened, surrendering the blissful illusion of safety and belonging with a sigh.

He dipped his head toward her and his mouth came down on hers. He kept the kiss light and gentle. The tension of his body suggested he restrained himself from doing anything more.

After a minute or two, he pulled back. He stared down at her before brushing a finger across her lips. "This has been one of the best days of my life. I hate for it to end, but I'm on duty tomorrow."

She took the hint and turned to unlock the apartment door. She entered, but the sound of his footsteps walking away didn't come until she'd fastened the chain and the deadbolt.

Sarah spent most of Sunday catching up on class work and studying, forcing herself not to dwell on the wonderful memories of the previous day. In the evening she joined her neighbors for the potluck supper held at Pam's place. It was a pleasant enough time and she talked with all of the neighbors except one. The resident of 1B traveled a great deal on business and was currently in Europe for several weeks.

Afterward, they talked about things they could do to improve security. Sarah was assigned to a committee to meet with the apartment management about a list of issues.

On Monday, she had a normal class day. Rob joined her for lunch again but didn't press her or act like anything other than a concerned friend.

No cars or persons followed her home that she could tell, fueling disappointment. She got back at three fifteen and knocked on Emily Petrie's door. The woman answered wearing a housedress and slippers, her hair in curlers.

"I'm here," Sarah said. "We'll need to leave in about twenty minutes. Can you be ready?"

Emily didn't respond for a moment. "I suppose so," she said at last. "I'll try."

Thirty minutes passed before she knocked on Sarah's door. They were running late but could still make it on time if traffic favored them. Amazingly, it did, and they got to the doctor's office only two minutes past their appointment time.

Sarah helped Emily fill out the paperwork and waited with her until she was called to the back. Sarah had brought her book-bag, so for the next hour she sat in the waiting room and studied.

After a while Emily came back out, accompanied by a nurse or aide.

"Are you the young lady who brought Mrs. Petrie?" the nurse asked. "She needs to have some tests, and they should really be done right away. We wondered if you could help her with transportation?"

"If we can schedule the appointment for late afternoon, I should be able to."

"Good. Come to the desk and let's see what we can set up."

The nurse got on the phone. After some back and forth they set up a time on Thursday afternoon. Emily protested at first, saying that was too soon and she wasn't sure she'd be ready, but the nurse insisted she couldn't wait any longer.

Emily continued to fret on the drive home. Sarah tried to be patient as she reiterated what the nurse had said about the dangers of waiting.

"I'm going to call tomorrow and re-schedule it," Emily said.

Sarah almost lost it. "Don't do that."

"Yes, I've decided. I can't do it this week. I can't. Next week will be soon enough."

"No, it won't," Sarah said. "Not according to the nurse."

"It's my decision to make, and I've made it. *Next* week."

Sarah kept quiet after that. Arguing further would do nothing but drive the woman deeper into her refusal.

They got back to the apartment block after six. Emily turned toward her door, saying she'd talk to Sarah later.

Sarah reached to put her key in the lock, but the door shifted inward before the key went into the hole. She pulled back, but the panel swung open at her touch anyway.

Her gut twisted and a groan escaped. "Oh, no. Please, no."

Chapter 10

Emily turned around. "What is it?

Sarah stared at her living room. "Someone broke in. And it looks like they've trashed the place." She reached into her purse and fumbled around until she found her cell phone. "No, don't go in," she told Emily, who had taken a step toward the door. "And don't touch anything. I'm calling the police."

She had Jay's number on speed dial now, a good thing since her hands shook so badly she might not have been able to press the small buttons in the right order otherwise.

"Christianson. Sarah?"

"Yes. Jay…" She paused for a moment, struggling to hold back a sob. "Someone broke into my apartment while I was gone. They smashed things up."

"What happened?"

She told him about taking her neighbor to the doctor and her suspicions about the door.

"Are you safe? Anyone still in there?"

"Doesn't look like it."

"Can you go and stay with your neighbor? Lock the doors until someone gets there. I'm having a unit dispatched to your place right now."

It reminded Sarah of the night the men had invaded her apartment. Probably the same ones had done this. Jay had said and done almost the same things too.

"I'll be with my neighbor until they get here."

"Don't let anyone go in or touch anything. I'm on my way."

"Okay. One thing… I don't think they touched the painting. It's still on the wall."

"Good. Sarah, are you in your neighbor's apartment yet?"

"No."

"In. Now. You don't know for sure someone isn't still in your place, waiting for you to be alone."

"Oh." She turned to Emily, who still watched her. "Can we go in your place? And lock the door?"

"Sure."

Once they were inside, she told Jay, "I'm in apartment 1C. We'll stay here until the police arrive."

"I'll tell them to knock on that door. I'm getting ready to leave too. Don't open the door until the cops identify themselves. Okay?"

"Okay."

He hung up.

Emily had wandered off to the kitchen. "I'm making coffee," she said. "You look like you need some."

"I do." Sarah collapsed into a chair, fighting nausea. They'd broken into her apartment. Probably searching for the elusive "key." And smashed up her things. She'd caught a quick glimpse of debris all over the floor. Her books lying there, pages torn out and strewn around. A bookshelf tipped on its side. God, they'd probably gone through the drawers in her bedroom… Was her underwear scattered around in there?

Emily brought a cup of coffee. "I put sugar and milk in it. I hope you like it that way." She held out a fragile porcelain cup on a matching and equally fragile saucer.

Sarah took it, willing her hand to keep from shaking. "That's fine. Thank you."

"Drink. You look like you're about to faint."

She felt that way, too. She took a careful sip. The coffee was lukewarm and way too sweet. How many spoonfuls of sugar had the woman put in? Still, it was liquid and bracing, so she drank it. She hadn't had any dinner yet and it helped fill the hollow spots in her stomach.

Emily had put a couple of small sandwiches on the side of the saucer, and Sarah forced herself to eat those as well.

As she finished the second one, a knock sounded on the door, followed by a loud male voice.

"Police officers."

Emily didn't have a peephole, so Sarah opened the door a crack. A man and woman, both in uniform, stood there. The man held up a badge where she could see it.

"CMPD, ma'am."

She opened the door to them.

"You're the lady who reported the break-in?" he asked.

Sarah nodded. She told them about coming home and finding the door open and then waited with Emily while the two officers went in to her apartment to make sure the intruders had indeed left.

Another pair of officers arrived, followed shortly by Jay, who showed his badge to the cops already there and consulted with them for a couple of minutes. He joined her in the hall, watching people tramp in and out of her apartment. His strong solid presence relieved her fear, letting other emotions bubble to the surface. Right then it didn't feel much like *her* apartment at all. The shock had started to wear off and anger roused to take its place. A sense of violation and abuse twisted her stomach into knots. An urge to strike back at someone stirred.

"Are you all right?" Jay asked her.

She dragged her thoughts back to reality and sucked in a long breath while struggling for calm. "Not hurt."

He put an arm around her shoulders and squeezed. "This isn't going to be easy for you, but you need to look at the apartment and see if anything is missing."

"From the brief glimpse I got, it might be hard to tell."

"It might, but you need to try. Particularly if anything valuable was taken."

She laughed harshly. "I don't own anything valuable. Well, a couple of pieces of jewelry maybe. My mother's desk. The laptop, but I had that with me. I don't think there's anything else in there that would be worth more than a couple of dollars."

"Still you need to take a look."

"I know. I'm just preparing myself. Like getting ready for a visit to the dentist."

* * * *

Sarah held herself stiffly, as if one wrong move would shatter her brittle control. Jay's heart twisted. He wished he could take her in his arms and tell her everything would be all right. But he couldn't follow either impulse. This was neither the time nor place for the first, and the second might well be a lie.

She straightened her spine, took a last drink from the coffee cup she held, and handed it back to the older woman standing beside her. In the tight-fitting jeans and dark blue sweater, she looked slender, almost fragile. Her long dark hair was pulled back away from her face and tucked behind her ears, giving her the air of a teenager. But the expression on her face showed more maturity than any teenager he knew--and most adults, too--as she steeled herself to do something she dreaded.

They walked across the hall and through the open door to her apartment. One of the uniformed officers joined them in the living room and another one came from her bedroom.

"Looks like they cut a pane out of the bedroom window," the latter said. "Reached in and undid the lock."

"Sounds like the burglar used the same modus as last time, just picked a better hour for this attempt," Jay said. "Still, this couldn't have been quiet. The walls are plaster and look pretty thick, so they might not let much sound out once he was inside."

"The man next door is out of the country right now," Sarah said. Her tone sounded hollow and too flat.

She scanned the floor of the living room while Jay made his own visual sweep. One of her bookshelves had been completely dismantled, the shelves removed, books strewn around and the unit upended. The other one still stood upright but had been pulled out from the wall with most of its contents also scattered.

An odd sound, half moan and half squeak, came from her. He followed her glance to where her mother's antique desk had stood. Its single drawer lay upside down on the floor. The desk itself sat on its side with two legs and a piece of the body broken off. The top, with its double row of cubbyholes, had come apart at one corner. She went over and picked up a piece, studying the jagged edge of the wood.

"Please don't touch any more than you have to," the officer said.

Sarah looked up at him and nodded. She put down the piece with a sigh.

Jay's chest got tight as he watched her survey the remains of everything she owned. He hurt for her. Her expression remained fixed, but her lips trembled.

"Can you tell if anything's missing?" he asked.

"I don't see anything obvious." Her gaze fell on the music box Vince had given her. Like most of her things, it had been broken, the box smashed and the mechanism lying naked on the floor.

She moved toward the bedroom. A chill breeze blew in through the open window. Jay followed her. Clothes had been dragged from drawers and tossed everywhere. She glanced in the closet where about half the items had been pulled off the hangers. Others hung askew. Shoes, sweaters, belts, a hat, and gloves lay in a heap at the bottom.

Only an occasional quiver of a lip or convulsive series of blinks betrayed her feelings. Her small dresser drew her next. Its drawers hung open, with bits of lace and silk clinging to the sides. She glanced into the top drawer and then dove for the pile of things on the floor at the side. She stood moments later, holding a jewelry box. The bottom had been broken out, leaving ragged splinters hanging off the sides. She scanned the floor again and got down on her hands and knees to gather a handful of chains, rings, and bracelets. She studied the group and searched again until she found the necklace with the blue stone.

"Doesn't look like they were after my jewelry. Nothing much is gone as far as I can tell. A couple of pieces I can't find, but I'll bet they're around somewhere." She held up the necklace. "If they didn't take this, though, they weren't interested in stealing valuables."

"I think it's safe to surmise this wasn't a routine burglary." Jay left Sarah's side to join the other cops and explain briefly the connection to the murder of Vince Capelli. They promised him the evidence people were on the way.

He went back to Sarah. "Pack an overnight bag and gather up anything valuable you don't want to leave in the apartment."

She gave him a blank look. "Not a hotel again."

"No."

She waited, but he wasn't ready to tell her what he planned. He wasn't sure it was a good idea, but he couldn't let her face the evening alone.

He didn't want to be by himself, either. He'd had a hell of a day already. Two new cases, another meeting with the sergeant, his and Sam's review of this case and their realization they'd run out of leads to pursue, and now this. Not likely, but if evidence could find a clue--a fingerprint, something they'd dropped, anything--it might provide a break.

While she scavenged clothes from the floor to put in the bag, he went back across the hall to retrieve her purse and backpack from her neighbor. The woman quizzed him about what was going on and where he was going to take Sarah. He said as little as possible, just telling her he'd keep Sarah safe.

"Can we go in there?" the woman asked. "To her apartment? I'd like to help do some cleaning up. I know some of the others here would, too. Sarah's such a sweetheart. It's a shame someone seems to have it in for her. She shouldn't have to come back to take care of all this by herself. It would be easier for her if most of the mess was gone by then."

Jay agreed but explained she'd have to wait until the police were finished investigating the place. He promised to have someone tell her when they could do it.

The evidence tech arrived. Jay consulted with the man, making sure he understood the importance of a thorough check of the apartment. By the time he'd talked with the other officers, explaining what he needed from them and why, Sarah had brought her case into the living room.

She gave him a small, sad smile and glanced at her backpack and purse. "Thanks for retrieving that."

He nodded. "Ready? Let's go."

"Wait. One more thing." She crossed the room and took down the painting he'd given her. "This comes with me."

When they finished stowing her things in the trunk and were in his car, she asked again, "Where are we going? Where am I staying?"

"For tonight, with me."

"With you?" Astonishment showed in her wide eyes and open mouth.

"Would you feel safer with one of your neighbors?" He tried to make it sound like a genuine offer.

"No."

He turned out of the parking lot and headed toward his condo. "Can you think of any place else you'd feel safer?"

That took a bit more thought but after a couple of moments she repeated, "No. But is it a good idea for you?"

"I don't know. It could be professional suicide. Personally…hard to tell. Except I know it's the right thing to do. This is not a night for you to be alone."

"Jay…" Her voice broke up.

He turned toward her just as the rays of a street lamp fell on her face. Tears glistened on her cheeks.

"I don't want you to take such a risk with your career. Take me to a hotel. I can handle it. I've…" She stopped to sniffle and wipe her eyes. "I'm sorry. I try not to be a sniveling little weakling."

"Sarah, you're the farthest thing I know from a sniveling weakling. Everyone has emotional letdowns. Even the strongest people. They just time it differently from the weak ones. The strong people of the world do what they have to do and don't let things overwhelm them to the point of becoming nonfunctional. They indulge the emotions when they're finally free to do so, like you're doing now."

She drew in a shaky breath. "Thanks. I told you before I try hard not to do self-pity. But I can't help wondering sometimes why God or fate or whatever seems to have it in for me. Every time I think I'm over the worst and starting to pick up the pieces again, it kicks me back to the bottom of the ladder."

"I don't know. It doesn't seem fair. Some people get a nice easy ride through life, while others struggle. I have no idea why. When I'm in danger of slipping into poor-me mode, though, I try to remember all the people in the world who have it much worse than I do. People who've lost their entire families and everything they own to natural disasters or war. People who watch their children die of starvation. People with long-term crippling illnesses. Things like that. It's not a cure, just perspective."

She was quiet for a while.

He drove into the parking lot of his section of condos. "Sarah? I wasn't belittling all the hard knocks you've taken. You've had more than your share."

She turned toward him and shook her head gently. "No, I know. And you sound like someone who's slid partway down that slippery slope yourself."

He laughed harshly. "Not partway down. All the way. And rolled in the mud at the bottom for a bit, too."

"What it did it take to get you out?"

"An intervention. Sam and my brother and a couple of others got together and told me quit wallowing in self-pity and get back to work. They pointed out I had a chance to do some good things in my job, to bring a bit of justice to the world, and I was wasting it. I got good and mad at them for a while, and then I realized they were right so I cleaned up my act."

He parked the car, and they spent the next few minutes on the logistics of getting her and her baggage up the steps to his second story unit and inside. After sweeping aside some of the extra stuff he'd dumped on the bed in his guest room, he put her bags in there and showed her where the guest bathroom was along with the linens and such.

Jay went to the kitchen and opened the refrigerator. "I haven't had dinner yet. Are you hungry?"

She wandered toward the kitchen and stopped in the doorway. A good thing. Two people in the space would make it crowded. "Yes. I only had a couple of little sandwiches a neighbor gave me."

"Looks like you have your choice of gourmet fare." He checked a cabinet. "Chicken noodle soup out of a can or an omelet made with whatever I can scrounge up. Actually I do a pretty mean omelet."

"Then definitely an omelet. Can I help? I'm not much of a cook, but I can chop veggies or something."

"Can you beat eggs?"

"At what? Monopoly? Probably. Poker? Probably not."

Laughter bubbled up from a too-long-unused part of his heart. "You couldn't beat an egg at poker? They're terrible bluffers." He reached down to pull an omelet pan from a drawer.

"I beg to differ. That shell gives them a definite advantage. No telling what's going on inside it."

"Point. But it's a brittle shell. Easy to poke holes and peek in."

"But really gooey and slippery once you get in there."

He laughed again. "Think you could herd a few of those slippery little suckers into a bowl?" He set the bowl and a carton that held five eggs on the table. He found a whisk in the drawer. "With this you can conquer the world. Or at least a few eggs."

"As long as they don't gang up on me," she said. "You may be overestimating my competence."

"I doubt it. You've done some cooking, surely?"

"I've done some. I'm just not good at it."

She showed more skill with the eggs than she claimed. If she took out some of her aggression on the helpless yolks, he could hardly blame her.

He turned his attention to the stove where the butter sizzled in the pan. "Set the table?" He took the bowl from her and nodded to the drawer holding forks and spoons.

By the time she had that done, the eggs had cooked firm and the cheese melted. He slid the omelet onto a plate, divided it in two, pulled a bottle of Chardonnay out of the fridge, and grabbed a mismatched pair of wine glasses from the cabinet.

"You're a good cook," she said after she'd taken a few bites.

Praise from her could go to his head if he didn't take care. "Not really, but I've learned to do a pretty decent omelet."

"How did you learn?"

"Trial and error. Practiced until I got it right. Did that mostly because I get in from work so pooped I don't have the energy to do more than fry up a couple of eggs or warm up a can of something."

"I do pretty well warming up canned soup, too," she said. "I can also toast bagels without burning too many of them and heat frozen meals in a microwave. Oh and decant canned fruit cocktail into a pretty bowl."

"Can you boil eggs?"

"Of course."

"Hard boiled and soft boiled?"

"There's a difference?"

"Rumor has it." He took a sip of the wine and couldn't help staring at her. The light glittered off her sleek, dark hair. He doubted she had any idea how sexy she looked each time she put a bite of omelet in her mouth and sucked it off the fork.

"Soft-boiled eggs sound yucky anyway," she said. The words were thin and a bit breathless.

"Not arguing. What about salads?"

"Good there. I can shred lettuce with the masters. Grate carrots, even chop up tomatoes."

He raised an eyebrow. "What about the dressing?"

"Kraft offers a nice selection, and I'm handy at pouring out of the bottle."

"Can you do it without getting little drips all over the place?"

"Most of the time."

"You beat me then. I always make a mess."

Once they were done, he rounded up the plates and put them in the sink. He grabbed the bottle of wine. "We'll be more comfortable in the living room."

She nodded and followed him. Jay turned on the gas logs in the fireplace to help dispel some of the autumn chill. He generally kept the heat turned down low since he spent so little time there.

They each took one of the two chairs that faced the fireplace and sipped in silence for a while. He'd flipped off the dining nook light and hadn't turned on any others, so the gas logs provided the only illumination. Shadows flickered across Sarah's face, driven by the glow from the fire.

After a while, she said, "You know it's weird, because it was nothing really, compared to what came after it, but the day was already going pretty badly even before I saw my apartment." She told him about Emily Petrie and the woman's determination not to keep the doctor's appointment they'd made.

"I get the impression there's something badly wrong. The nurse seemed to think it very important she get those tests as soon as possible. But I didn't know how to convince her when she decided not to do it."

"You can't force other people to do things they don't want to. You can try to convince them, but if they won't do it, you have to accept it. It's the old free will conundrum."

"I know, but it's annoying. Anyway, it added a bit more frustration to another seriously bad day to put in my trophy case of bad days."

"Not the worst one ever, though."

She held her wineglass up, between her face and the fire, and swirled the liquid. "No. Several candidates for that, but I think the absolute worst was the day I found out about Barbara's cancer. My mother had just died two months before. I felt like I'd been stomped on and beaten down into the ground. But I couldn't show it. I had to be strong for Barbara. I had to convince myself and her she could beat the odds."

"She didn't though," he said.

"No." Sarah hesitated and swallowed hard. "For a while I thought she might. She seemed to be responding to the chemo, and the cancer did go into remission for a while. About a year. Not long enough." She looked up at him with tears glittering in her eyes. "What was your worst day?"

He curled his fingers around the stem of the wineglass and fought against the way his nerves tightened and stomach roiled. He'd all but invited her to ask, so he couldn't blame her for accepting the invitation. Didn't make it any easier to talk about, though.

He tried out and rejected several ways of easing toward it. She sat quiet and patient while he sought the words. Bald and direct was really the only way he could go with it.

"My worst day ever would be the day my wife killed herself." He stared into his wineglass, unwilling to face the shock and horror in her eyes.

For a moment she didn't say anything, then she asked, "What happened?"

The words were quiet, with no hint of condemnation or anything other than sympathetic curiosity.

He drained the wine in his glass, poured some more, and topped hers off as well. "It's a long story."

"We're not going anywhere." She accepted the refilled glass from him, her dark eyes serious and concerned.

He took a mouthful of wine and let it sit on his tongue for a moment, savoring the smooth tartness. "I met Theresa about seven years ago. I was still riding patrol." His memories of the night itself had started to fade. He couldn't remember what the weather had been like or what else had happened that day. "Someone called in a report of an injured young woman on the sidewalk in a middle class neighborhood. They thought she might have fallen and hurt herself.

"I got the call. It wasn't hard to find her since a crowd had gathered. She'd definitely fallen and banged her head. But my nose told me there was more to it than that, so I followed the ambulance guys to the hospital. The doctors confirmed my suspicion. She had a blood alcohol way past intoxicated. I wrote up the report and talked to her family."

He closed his eyes for a moment as he steeled himself for another onslaught of pain. "She was twenty-one. From a broken family. Mother was an alcoholic. Theresa had a job as a receptionist, but she got involved with a rough crowd and sort of lost her way. Drinking too much. Maybe doing drugs. I spent a long time talking to her when she finally got coherent again. Something about her got to me. I-- I was still gung-ho for helping people at that time. Plus she was attractive and I was susceptible."

"You got involved with her."

He nodded. "Just as a friend at first. I thought I could help her get back on a more healthy path for her life. It seemed to work too, for a while. We started dating and then… She got pregnant."

"And being the honorable man you are, you married her."

He shrugged. "I don't know so much about honor. But it seemed like the right thing to do. We had a few good months. Then…" He struggled to grasp and express it. After all these years, he still didn't really understand what had happened. "The bottom kind of fell out. She got all wonky and began fighting with me, screaming at me, and she'd go off and shut herself in her room for a day or two. Wouldn't do anything at all. I thought it was just hormones from the pregnancy, and that probably contributed. But after a while I knew it wasn't normal, that something was badly wrong. She'd disappear for days, and I couldn't find her, then she'd come back looking like she'd been dragged through the mud and run over by a truck. When I asked where she'd been, she said she'd been visiting friends. She'd never tell me who they were."

He stopped long enough for another sip. "Well, hell, I'm a cop. It took longer than it should've, mostly because I didn't want to see it, but I did finally realize she was doing drugs again. When I confronted her, she even admitted it. I tried to get her into rehab or a twelve-step. She said she would and then refused to do anything. I dragged her to a counselor and she sat through the sessions glaring at me and refusing to say a word. I cut off her money, and she started shoplifting things and fencing them. I ran out of ideas. I considered getting her arrested. I even toyed with having her committed but couldn't bring myself to do it. Now… Heck, I doubt it would have worked, but I wish I'd at least tried."

He held the wineglass up, rolling it in his hand. Light from the gas logs threw odd reflections off it, spraying crazy refractions over walls and furniture. He breathed in the fruity aroma of the liquid. A faint hiss came from the fireplace, and the refrigerator clunked through a cooling cycle. Sarah kept quiet until he felt ready to go on.

"She miscarried at just past six months. No one said this, but I'm sure the drugs contributed to it. After that, things went downhill so fast it was over almost before I realized it was happening. I came home from work

a couple of months later and found her on the floor. She'd overdosed."
He clenched his fingers too tightly around the stem of the wineglass, but
then loosened his grip before he shattered it. "I have no idea if it was
an accident or deliberate. I don't know that it matters. She'd still been a
pretty girl when I first met her, despite the excesses. By the time she died,
a year later, she was a mess. It took me a long time to accept I did the best
I could, and you can't help someone who doesn't want to be helped."

"Like I can't force Emily Petrie to go to the doctor if she doesn't want
to. But it doesn't seem right when you know someone is harming herself."

Whether the effects of the wine began to spread through him, or if just
telling her about his sad, sordid past had unloaded some of the burden,
relief began to filter through him. She didn't seem to judge him the sort
of failure he'd long considered himself. "It may not seem right, but it is.
People have the freedom to make their own choices as long as they're
capable of it. Heck, even if they're not, there's only so much you can do."

"I suppose so." She reached across to take his hand. "It really tore you
up, didn't it?"

The simple touch of her fingers set his blood racing. "It took a while
to get over it. I learned a hard lesson about not mixing my personal and
professional lives."

But here I am, doing it again.

She stared at him, her dark eyes wide and luminous. She was the
prettiest woman he'd ever seen. Warmer and more attractive than Theresa
had ever been. His body responded. Desire sent blood rushing to his groin
and made his pulse rise.

By sliding forward on the chair, he could reach over and pull her closer.
"You're taking a risk with me, aren't you?" she said.

His mind said *yes*. His body said *who cares*? The body won the
argument. He put both hands on her cheeks, enjoying the sleek feel of her
soft, smooth skin. "A small one."

It *wasn't* a small one, though. It was a huge one, probably a disastrous
one. Right then he didn't care.

She didn't contradict him, though her raised eyebrows suggested doubt.
He dipped his head, pressed his mouth to hers, and the doubt cleared. Her
lips parted for him, and he swept his tongue into the hot, slick depths of
her mouth. She took him in, accepting him, and fire broke out in his groin,
spreading heat all up and down his skin.

Their tongues danced, meeting, touching, backing away, touching
more surely, and then winding around each other. He withdrew a little

and swiped his mouth across her lips, nipped gently at her lip and rubbed the place to soothe the small pain.

She reached for his shoulders and clung there, fingers digging in.

Urgent, pressing need blotted out thought. Only sensation existed. The feel of Sarah's skin against his, the gentle floral aroma that surrounded her, the taste of her mouth, and the soft hum of desire percolating from deep in her throat combined to rouse the animal sleeping inside. It roared hunger and warning. A surge of possessiveness wove through the desire that set him aflame. Sarah was his woman, his love, his life. Whatever happened, he'd fight with everything he had for her.

He pulled her closer and tugged until she came out of her chair and ended up sitting across his lap. She didn't resist. Once on him, she leaned her head against his shoulder, without drawing her mouth from his. Her hair spilled down his chest and over his arm where he'd rolled up the sleeve of his shirt.

Her sweater was in his way, so he worked his hands beneath it. Her gasp as his fingers rested on the satiny skin of her stomach broke their mouths apart. He kissed his way across her cheek to just below her ear and continued down the line of her throat. When Sarah moaned, his heartbeat ratcheted up another notch.

As he brushed his lips down her neck, his fingers crept up her stomach until they encountered the fabric barrier of a bra. Following some awkward maneuvering to get the cups pushed aside, he reached her breasts. He paused, waiting for her to resist or pull back. It didn't happen.

He explored her breasts, gliding fingertips over silken skin and graceful curves, seeking the places that seemed most sensitive. She gasped and jumped when he brushed across her nipple, so he did it again. And again.

The crotch of his pants grew uncomfortably tight, but he feared that if he moved to relieve the pressure, he'd explode on the spot. His exploration of her body provided compensation for the discomfort. Sarah had breasts of a perfect size and shape to fit a man's hands, so responsive he'd never want to stop trying to find new ways to make her gasp and squirm.

Her breath heaved in and out on harsh pants, and she dug her fingers into his back as he played with her. When she lifted a hand from his shoulder and put it on his chest, little tongues of fire settled in where she touched, even through the fabric of the shirt. Then she started on the buttons.

Breath clotted in his chest. He'd never felt anything like this. When she made a gap large enough to squeeze her hand through, her fingertips burned like brands against his flesh, marking her ownership of his heart.

She swiped her fingers across his chest and over a nipple. A groan forced its way past the obstruction in his throat.

His erection strained toward her, demanding to claim its rightful place inside her. She'd be hot and slick and sweet, wanting him, needing him, maybe as badly as he needed her.

In one motion, he lifted the hem of her sweater and drew it over her head. He fumbled with the clasp on the back of the bra but finally got it loose, pulled the straps down her arms, and tossed the filmy mass aside.

God help me…

"You're beautiful," he said, when he could talk again. "The most beautiful woman I've ever seen." His gaze flicked between her breasts and her face, unable to decide which pleased him more. Both treated him to glimpses of loveliness beyond anything he could possibly deserve.

But her face pulled into a worried frown. "Jay? You know I've… I'm not…"

"You're not a virgin."

Her head jerked in a sharp nod.

His hand stilled on her breast. "I kind of already figured that out."

"It doesn't bother you?"

He laughed harshly. "I'm not exactly a virgin myself."

"But you were married."

"And you were desperate and had only one asset to capitalize on. Besides, Theresa was pregnant when we got married. I'm in no position to cast stones."

She sighed. "Still, I wish things could be different. I wish I could be better…for you."

"You couldn't possibly be better."

Apparently he said the right thing. She leaned against him and the hand resting on his chest resumed that rubbing thing that was driving him crazy. Her breasts called to him, so he leaned down and let his lips slide over that incredibly soft, sleek skin.

So much blood pooled in his groin, the pressure hurt, especially when she started wriggling on him.

He had to stop and pull back a bit. "Sarah, I can't… I'm on the verge of exploding."

She reached for the button on his slacks. "Then let's do something about it."

Unfortunately, before she even got the zipper down, his cell phone buzzed. The sound sliced through the fog of desire, making them both jump. Sarah slid off his lap onto the floor, though he reached and grabbed her hand to keep her from hitting too hard.

He wanted to ignore it. It was probably his brother or parents, but it could be work as well. Although he'd told Sam he wanted to take the rest of the night off, they could still call him if something important came up. "I've got to take this," he said.

She nodded and backed away. He drew a breath, pushed to his feet, and went to get the phone. In his state of arousal, any move required a painful effort. He cursed up one side and down the other, though only to himself, when he got to the phone and saw the caller ID number. Will. He debated not taking it and going back to Sarah, but she had already gathered up her bra and sweater and was putting them back on. Shit.

"Yeah?" he said.

"Somebody's grumpy," Will said.

"You would be, too. What is it?"

"Am I interrupting work or pleasure?"

"Take your pick."

"Drat. Sorry. Just wanted to check with you on next week. Lisa's birthday dinner on Saturday."

"I'm off. Barring the unforeseen, I'll be there."

"Good enough. Back to your regularly unscheduled normal programming."

"I wish," Jay muttered. He ended the call and turned to Sarah, now fully clothed again. "I'm sorry."

"It's probably just as well. We kind of lost it there."

"Not for the interruption."

"Oh." She gave him a wry smile. "You know... I'm not. Except I know this makes things harder for you. I am sorry about that." She drained the last sip of wine in her glass. "I'd better get to bed. It's been a long day and I have classes tomorrow. Could you drop me off at my apartment so I can pick up my car, or should I call a cab?"

"I'll drop you off. What time do you need to be there?" The words came out harsher than he intended, frustration taking its toll on him.

"About eight thirty should get me to campus on time."

"I'll be ready to leave at eight."

"Thank you." She turned to go. "I have a lot to thank you for, and I don't know how to do it. I appreciate your...helping me pick up the pieces."

"My motives aren't all altruistic. You're our only link to whoever killed Vince Capelli. One way or another, it's pretty obvious you have the key and someone else wants it."

"Unless they found what they were looking for in my apartment."

"The way they tore things up, I don't think so. That looked like a lot of frustration. And it didn't stop anywhere. If they had found it, they'd've quit and lit out. But everything was torn up, every drawer and cabinet emptied, every closet ransacked. If I were a betting man, I'd lay odds they didn't find it."

"And what do you make the odds *we*'ll ever find it?"

He hesitated, wanting to say something reassuring. But she already knew. "Not great. But it does narrow things down."

"To what?"

"I'm not sure. Maybe just to you. And I'm not sure what that means, but we're both too tired to sort it out tonight." And his brainpower was still mostly being sucked away to points south.

She nodded and said "Good night" before going into the guest room and closing the door.

Sleep eluded him for a while. He couldn't escape feeling the jaws of some giant trap were closing in on him.

Sarah Martin was the first woman who'd interested him since Theresa's death, but he doubted they'd have much chance to build anything together. They needed a miracle to find who really killed Vince Capelli now.

Chapter 11

Sarah woke at dawn as usual. It took a moment to orient herself to the room around her. She'd just begun to get used to the apartment and now she was…in Jay Christianson's guest room. In the increasing light, she glanced around the space, smiling at the abundant proof the room belonged to a man. No woman would put a bicycle in the corner leaning up against the wall, or hang a topological map as the only picture. Shelves lined another wall, holding an assortment of books, sports gear, trophies, electronics in various stages of dismemberment, and camping equipment.

A stack of sports magazines sat on the floor, where he'd moved them from the bed yesterday, and a basketball rested atop a trash can too small for it to slide into. The dresser top held more mementos as well as a baseball mitt, a handful of coins, and…dear heaven. Was that a jockstrap?

She forced herself to get up and get in the shower. Since she hadn't done any homework yesterday, she'd have to wing it in her early class and try to catch up before the afternoon. By the time she'd dressed, brushed out her hair, and done makeup, she smelled coffee brewing.

She followed the aroma to the kitchen. Jay stuffed a couple slices of bread into the toaster and got butter and jam from the refrigerator.

"Don't do big breakfasts," he said. "Hope you don't mind."

"Not a problem. As long as there's coffee, I'm good."

He poured her a cup and stopped to stare for a moment as he handed it to her. "You're looking better this morning. You slept well?"

"I did." She found that surprising. No nightmares. "And I'm ready to tackle the business of rebuilding yet again."

She couldn't help but stare at him. Bright light poured in through the windows, reflecting in his blue-gray eyes, delineating his tall, lean body. It picked out the threads of silver in his dark brown hair and showed light creases in his narrow face, including hints of the grooves around his mouth when he smiled.

He might not be the most handsome man she'd ever seen, but he was certainly the most attractive. Strength of character showed on his face, in the set of his jaw and the serious lines around his eyes. She wanted to kiss him again.

Instead, she turned around to find the sugar for the coffee. "Do you think I'll be able to get back in my apartment today to start cleaning up?"

"I don't know. I'll check with the evidence people this morning and let you know."

"If they're not, I'll go to a hotel."

"We'll talk about that if it's necessary."

She just nodded and let it go. He asked about her schedule over their quick breakfast of toast, juice and coffee. Once they were done, she gathered up her things and put them back into her bag.

"I wonder how much can be salvaged," she said once they were in his car again, headed back to her apartment.

"Probably more than you think."

"I hope you're right."

"A lot of it was just mess that can be cleaned up."

"You'd think after the night…after what happened to Vince, nothing could make me feel that shocked, that violated again."

"Paper cuts still sting, even after you've been stabbed."

"This was more like a gut punch than a paper cut."

"I think our metaphors just got mixed."

"I need another cup of coffee before I can keep my metaphors in a row."

He took his gaze off the road for a brief grin at her, flashing the lovely creases in his cheeks.

Sarah's heart twisted in her chest. It was stupid. It was dangerous. It would probably bring more pain. But she couldn't do anything about it now. She was in love with him.

The odds didn't look good for any kind of future with him. Could she do anything about that? Were there any leads she hadn't pursued? Any place Vince might have hidden a key she hadn't thought of yet? Anything he'd given her?

If "the key" wasn't something Vince had given her, it must have been something he'd told her. She'd just begun the mental review of recent conversations with Vince when they arrived at her building. It looked quiet, with only a few cars still sitting in the lot and no one else around. Yellow crime-scene tape stretched across the closed door to her apartment.

Jay parked next to her car and transferred her bag to its trunk. "I'll call to let you know about where to go this afternoon," he promised. "Sarah?"

She unlocked her car and turned back to him.

"Be careful. Please." Strain pulled the muscles of his face taut. "They didn't find what they were looking for, and that doesn't leave them too many options. None of them good for you. In fact, I'd feel happier if I took you back to my place and you stayed there. Would you consider going back? Right now?"

She wanted to. She wanted to stay with him forever, to hide in the warmth of his arms, the safety of his presence. But safety of any kind was an illusion in the circumstances. Not doing anything was possibly even more dangerous than whatever else she might try. And hiding away might actually rob her of what little chance she had.

"No. I get your worry, but I can't live my life that way," she said. "Besides, there is no safety for me. I'm likely damned if I do and just as damned if I don't. If I'm going down, I'd rather go down swinging."

"Sarah, don't--" The concern in his eyes curled its way into her heart. It warmed her to know he wanted to protect her.

He drew a breath that expanded his chest before he let it out. "I'm trying to do as much swinging for you as I can, but it might not be enough. And I admire that you don't want to hide. Really. So I'm trying to restrain my primitive, protect-the-little-lady instincts. But at least be careful, okay? Don't do anything foolish. No walking down deserted alleys or driving out on lonely roads."

She grinned at him. "I promise I won't."

He bent forward and for a moment she thought he might kiss her again. She waited for it. Instead, he turned sharply and got back into his own car. He waved once as he drove away.

She missed him moments after he'd left. But she had things to do, so she drove to campus.

She had an hour and a half between classes at lunchtime, and she didn't want to meet Rob, so instead of going to the cafeteria, she used the break to find a quiet corner, still in plain sight, where she could make a few phone calls.

The call to Marc revealed he'd learned nothing new that would help her. Her next call went to Vince's attorney, Craig Winthorpe. He wouldn't talk about most of Vince's business, saying it was privileged information and he honored that even though his client was no longer alive. What he would discuss, Vince's investments and his consulting on currency exchanges, she already knew. When she asked the lawyer about keys, he claimed to know nothing at all.

Some of Vince's friends might have some insight into his business. The police would have already questioned them, but she might get something new. She opened up her computer to search for them. Unfortunately "Joe Williams" was so generic she couldn't narrow down the hundreds of references in the area to figure out which might be the right one. She found Anthony Rysdale easily enough, but he hung up before she got Vince's name completely out of her mouth. When she tried again, he didn't answer. She left a voice mail, hoping he might listen to the whole thing and respond.

At a loss for other names to contact, she went to the campus store, where she bought a fresh notebook and a wrapped sandwich from the vending machine. While eating the sandwich, she did her assignment for the next class, and once that was finished, she tried to review and write down things she could remember Vince saying to her. She'd determined to write down everything, no matter how trivial, but had just started when she had to leave to make her next class.

Her phone rang as she walked across campus.

"You can go back to your apartment," Jay said. "I've arranged for a guy to fix the window later this afternoon. His name's Chris Newman. He knows to identify himself when he knocks on the door."

She thanked him and said goodbye as she went into the classroom building.

She barely listened to the professor and spent more time scribbling in her "Vince's Words" notebook than in the "Modern European History" one.

Rob caught up with her just outside the building and walked with her around the corner toward the parking lot.

"Sarah? Got a minute?"

She stopped and sighed but plastered a smile on her face. "Yes."

People streamed around them and one knocked into her. Rob nodded to a quieter area nearby, in a corner made by a brick building with a short wing jutting from its side. It was still in plain sight, so she went with him to get out of the way.

He licked his lips and drew in a long breath. "I have to tell you… When we met last year, I felt like there was something special between us. But when I found out about Vince, I backed off. Now he's gone and I…"

Rob moved in closer to her, crowding her back against the wall. "Don't you feel it, Sarah? When I'm with you, it's like there's some magic going on." He leaned down to kiss her.

Sarah let him do it, but she didn't move or respond. After a minute or two, he backed off. She put her arms on his to hold him off a little. "Rob? I don't want to hurt you, and I like you very much. But there's nothing more happening, and it won't. There's someone else. I don't know if I have any future with him. Right now, I don't know if I have a future with anyone. But this won't work."

She hated the pained look that ran across his face before he could hide it.

"Are you sure? Really?"

"I'm afraid so. But I value our friendship, if that can survive."

He stepped back. "I don't know, Sarah. I don't know if I can." He turned and walked away from her as another clump of people came around the corner.

Sarah got in behind them, following them to the parking lot. Because she spent so much time brooding over the scene with Rob as she drove home, it took her longer than it should have to realize a familiar blue car was behind her, staying several car-lengths back but making all the same turns she did.

Her heart did a curious flip and hard beat, and then settled into a rapid pounding. She considered places to pull over, where they'd have to pass. Not on this side road leading off campus. Too deserted. The highway would be better. There she could roll onto the shoulder without too much warning, assured of enough witnesses around to keep the guys in the car from trying anything ugly.

As long as they didn't try anything before she got there. Another car occupied the road not far ahead. Sarah pressed the accelerator to get closer and followed in its wake until they reached the intersection with the main road. As they stopped, she strained to see who was in the blue car behind. A tinted windshield defeated her, though she thought she could make out one form behind the wheel. She couldn't see a face.

She kept an eye on the car while she drove along the four-lane main road toward the highway, but the other driver seemed content to hang back and follow. Good. Her pursuer let another vehicle slip between them but it remained behind when she turned onto the highway.

She knew the spot she wanted, a place where the highway widened temporarily between two closely spaced exits. Don't slow down, she reminded herself when she realized she was easing up on the speed. She couldn't afford to give any hint of what she planned. She exerted all her willpower to keep from speeding up or changing lanes until she got past the first of the two exits.

After checking the rearview mirror to be sure no other cars were in the way, she braked hard and, without signaling, swerved to the right, streaking across the access lane onto the shoulder. The car behind veered too, but then the driver reconsidered and blew by.

Sarah watched intently as the car passed.

"Well, blast." Mud obscured all but the first letter of the license plate. It probably wouldn't help very much, unless they could search for a recent model Toyota Camry with "V" as the starting digit. Right. How many of those were on the road?

She shook herself out of the disappointment, signaled, and pulled back onto the highway. Not a good idea to hang around here. She remained hyper-alert as she continued home, hoping the other driver would wait for her to pass by again. Apparently not. No other vehicle accompanied her the rest of the way to her apartment.

She hammered on the steering wheel with a fist. Disappointment tightened her chest. She'd let her hopes rise when she'd seen the blue car. Now the frustration infuriated her. So many things she'd tried had come to nothing.

Sarah turned into the parking lot and tucked the car into its space. As she grabbed the handle to get out, she looked up in time to see the door to her apartment open. She'd already reached for her cell phone when the male half of the couple in apartment 1E emerged, carrying a trash bag. He looked up, noticed her, and turned to say something into the apartment. Emily Petrie poked her head out the door as Sarah put the phone back in her purse and got out of the car.

"What are you doing?" She stopped at the door.

Emily backed into her place again. Carlie was stacking books back on the bookshelf, which had been moved against the wall where it belonged. Her computer desk also stood upright. Sarah walked in and looked around. Most of the papers had been collected from the floor, the books organized, and the debris swept or vacuumed up. The pieces of her mother's desk were gone, probably in the nearest Dumpster.

Emily followed her in. "Your boyfriend told us it was okay. He said we shouldn't throw out anything that might possibly be fixed. He took a few things with him. The pieces of that pretty writing desk you had. I guess he thinks he can repair it or something."

Jay had taken the broken desk to fix? "Did he ask you to do this?"

Emily shook her head. "It was my idea. I asked him last night to let me know when we could get in here to work. Bad enough this happened to you. I knew it would be hard for you to have to clean it all up by yourself."

Her eyes burned. She fought to get words past her tight throat. "Nobody's ever done anything this thoughtful for me before. I... I can't tell you how grateful I am. I never expected this, but I appreciate it more than I can say."

"Well, it's been kind of good for us, too," Carlie said. "Made us more aware of how vulnerable we all are. How much we have to stay alert and keep our eyes open. Plus, it's kind of brought us together some. We have to look out for each other. That detective said you had no other family. So I guess we have to be one for you."

"Oh, my--" Sarah had to turn her face away. She was losing the fight against tears.

"Hey, it's all right," Emily said. "With the three of us working, it hasn't even taken very long. By the way, Carlie and I took care of getting your clothes put back away. Didn't think you'd want Rick here doing that. We let him handle sweeping up duties."

Rick looked at her, shrugged, and grinned. "Played hockey back in the day, so I swing a mean broom."

"I'm overwhelmed."

Rick looked around the room. "Couldn't rescue most of the pictures. Couple of the prints were all torn up."

"But the pictures of you and your family are okay." Carlie pointed to the photographs lying on a shelf. "Just need new frames."

"Wait."

Sarah went out to the car and got the painting Jay had given her. When she hung it back on the hook he'd installed, it worked its magic yet again, brightening up the apartment, bringing color and joy to the blank white walls. The same magic the man himself had brought into her life.

"Hey, that's nice," Emily said. "Pretty flowers."

"Yeah." Sarah smiled.

A knock sounded on the door.

"Chris Newman. Here to fix a broken window."

Sarah opened the door for him and showed him the window.

"Looks like someone cut right through it," he said.

"Yeah. They broke in. We're cleaning up the mess now."

While Newman worked on the window, Sarah and her neighbors finished putting things to rights as much as possible. When she did an inventory, she discovered she'd lost less than she expected. The inexpensive prints she'd had on the wall didn't survive, nor did a few of the dishes Jay had brought. Some of the books had pages mangled but not destroyed. The handle of one pot had broken off. Unfortunately, it was the one she used most, but it could be replaced. The figurines Vince had given her were gone, all broken.

If they hadn't been gifts from Vince she wouldn't have cared about the knick-knacks. She did regret the music box, but she'd seen enough of it the previous night to know it was beyond repair.

Sarah ordered pizza for everyone to thank them for the help.

When they all finally departed, she locked up behind them, spent an hour on classwork for the next day, and then started on the "Vince's Words" notebook again. She didn't think about or try to analyze the words. She just wanted to get down as much as possible.

After an hour or so she badly wanted to hear Jay's voice. She considered calling him to ask about the desk, but that was only an excuse, so she held off.

At nine-thirty, he called her. "I've got the pieces of your mother's desk. Will said he'd take a look and see if it could be fixed. He's good at that kind of thing."

After thanking him and asking him to pass the gratitude on to his brother, she told him about the car that followed her that afternoon.

"I'm not surprised you couldn't read the plate. Everything about these guys says professional," he said. "They wouldn't expose themselves that way."

Sarah sighed. "I suppose so. But I'd hoped... Anyway. I'm trying something else." She told him about the notebook.

"That's a great idea." He paused for a moment. "Are you okay there tonight by yourself?"

"I have great neighbors."

"I know. But they can only be so much help."

"You know I'd rather be staying with you. And you know it wouldn't be a good idea."

"It might actually be a really good time, but Sarah"--his tone changed drastically--"things are getting bad with our investigation. I'm getting a lot of pressure. It's starting to squeeze."

"To make an arrest?"

"Yeah. Any arrest."

"How bad is it? How much time do I have?"

"A week, at most. And we've got nothing. We've pursued every lead, every hint, everything. Whoever did this has covered his tracks thoroughly. You and your key are the only loose end."

"If you believe my story."

Another pause stretched out for a moment. Fear and tension made her queasy.

"Sarah, I do believe it. But that may not make any difference. Sam believes it too. Our sergeant might too, but you can't imagine the pressure he's under. It won't make any difference."

"I understand. But I've got midterm exams next week."

"Missing those would be the least of your problems."

"I know, but…"

"Don't think about it tonight. Work on the notebook. Okay? And I'm doing everything I can."

"I believe it. Jay, what--? No, forget it."

"What will I do?" He sighed. "What I have to."

"What's right. You'll do what's right. That's the man you are. The man I love."

He made an odd choked noise and then stayed silent for a moment. "God, Sarah. I don't know. I just don't know what I'll do. But I love you too."

"That's enough for me right now."

She had a mostly normal day the next day, except for the constant feeling of a sword looming over her head, poised to fall. Rob stayed away, probably licking his wounds. She spent every spare moment, including many she should have given to studying, writing in the Vince notebook. By the end of the day, she'd filled almost half of it.

No cars followed her home, and other than her spending some time talking to neighbors, nothing of any interest happened. Most of the following day stayed normal too.

Until she finished her last class and headed to the parking lot.

As she crossed the street that ran between the main part of the campus and the student parking lot, a blue car screamed out of a driveway nearby. It didn't slow down on the street but turned toward her and accelerated.

She froze. The car barreled down at her, swerving to the left to aim square at her.

Chapter 12

Sarah stared for a moment, and then scrambled to the nearer edge ahead. The car veered toward her. She jumped up onto the curb and raced across the narrow grass strip that separated the road from the parking lot. The blue Toyota followed, bumping over the curb and crossing the grass behind her. It closed on her as she looked desperately around for help. No one else was nearby. The lot held about a third of the cars that had parked there that morning, and the area directly in front of her was almost empty. Sarah veered to her left. The car had to take more space to make the turn and it gave her a couple of seconds.

Her own car was ten rows down with a large open expanse between her and it. She needed something closer to duck into. Only a single vehicle, a white Mercedes, stood close enough for her to reach easily. It could buy her a few more seconds. If the gods were merciful, it would be unlocked. She raced to it and collapsed against it, breathing hard. The door handle didn't give. Shit.

The blue car had turned on the asphalt of the half-empty lot. It headed toward her again, threatening to pin her against the side of the Mercedes. She dived to the rear, watching her pursuer veer again to follow her around.

Sarah tripped, fell, and slid along the asphalt, ripping her jeans and skinning her knees. Her jacket helped protect her elbows, though one cheek rubbed painfully along the ground as well. She scrambled to her feet and jumped up on the tail of the Mercedes. If the driver had a gun, she was too exposed. Shaking off her backpack, she rolled off the other side and ducked against the rear quarter panel. To get to her there, the Toyota had to make a wide turn. It gave her enough time to scoot to the front of the car and crouch there. What to do now? She couldn't stay here forever.

Two people appeared across the street and stopped to stare.

"Call the cops," Sarah screamed at them. Prayed that one of them had a cell phone and understood her.

She scanned the area. The blue car stood still, facing the Mercedes, waiting for her to make a move. A hundred yards or so to her left, two cars parked close together offered her a refuge between them the Toyota couldn't reach. Too far for her to get to, though, unless she could lure it into committing to another direction.

She took a moment to catch her breath and then ducked out to the right. *Take the bait, take the bait*, she prayed silently. After a moment they did. As soon as the car started rolling toward her, she reversed direction, ran past the front of the Mercedes, and shot across the open area toward the small cluster of parked cars. She didn't dare take time to look back or around. Tires squealed and the engine churned as the Toyota swiveled toward her. Gravel sprayed and the motor roared as it accelerated.

Sarah blessed the flat shoes she'd chosen to wear that morning. She ran faster than she'd ever thought she could. Even so, the car raced behind her, too close. Instead of continuing toward her target cluster of cars too far ahead, she made a sharp left and shot back toward the road. A row of trees stood directly in front but another fifty yards off. It wouldn't help her either. But on the other side of the street, the ground rose toward the main part of the campus. That could help her.

She zigged right and zagged left, which brought her out to the street. The Toyota veered with her, but took more time adjusting to her rapid changes of direction. Sarah looked left. A car approached from that direction, but she had time to get across the street ahead of it. She could use it though, if she waited a half second more.

The wait brought more reward than she'd anticipated. As the approaching vehicle got closer, the light bar on the top came into view. She stepped into the street. The blue Toyota started to follow, its front wheels charging onto the grass of the narrow strip. Then it braked sharply. The campus cop car slowed. The Toyota reversed onto the asphalt, wheeled hard to the right, and took off in the other direction.

"Miss?" An older man leaned out of the cop car as it pulled up. "Are you all right? We had a call about something going on here. Someone being chased by another car. That you?" He glanced after the Toyota as it screeched out of the parking lot, and then looked back to her. His scan took in her disheveled clothes, torn jeans, and scraped knees.

"Me." She leaned over. Her breath came in huge pants now that the danger had abated. Her pulse raced and sweat coursed down her temples. After taking a moment to collect herself, she explained about the car trying to hit her. The kid she'd screamed at to call the cops approached to ask how she was. He verified her story.

While the cop filled out a report, the boy retrieved her backpack from the Mercedes and handed it to her. The cop took her to the Student Health Center and completed his paperwork while a nurse applied antiseptic and bandages to her scrapes. Then he drove her back to her car and waited nearby, standing guard until she was settled in it and drove off.

Her hands shook on the steering wheel, but she controlled the reaction well enough to get home without further mishap. A small miracle. Deep inside her gut, fear met fury, and the two melded into an explosive mix. It churned inside her like acid, eating its way through any containment.

She pulled out the cell phone and called Jay.

"They tried to kill me."

"Hell. Are you all right?"

"Mostly." She told him what had happened and he promised to be at her apartment in fifteen minutes.

After stripping off the torn jeans, she got into a pair of softer slacks that didn't chafe the abraded places not covered by the bandages. A glance in the mirror showed little swelling at the scrape on her temple but it was starting to darken with unattractive blue-black blotches.

Jay got to her door in twelve minutes. He looked at her face, his expression tightening as he studied the scrape along her temple. "You're sure you're all right?" Anger lit sparks in his light eyes.

"Shaky but not really hurt. I'm just--furious." The emotion she'd been fighting coursed through her body in wave after wave of frustration. "I'm tired of this shit and furious about it and I don't know what to do. I want to do something to stop it. I want to get revenge on the guys who killed Vince and are tormenting me. But I don't know how."

"You're doing the only thing you can. The only thing likely to help. Try to figure out where and what that key is."

"I'm not having much success. It's only adding to the frustration. I want to do something more. Something more active. I hate having to take their harassment and assaults and…everything else, and not be able to do anything about it." She was starting to yell and forced herself to calm down. Her hands closed in tense fists and all her muscles tightened. "They killed Vince. *Killed him.* Now they're trying to kill me, too. And all I can do about it is write in a notebook? It's not working for me."

"I understand the frustration," he said. "Believe me. All too well. I'm just as frustrated. And I'm afraid I'm just as much at a loss to know what to do." He drew a breath. "Have you eaten? Let's go get some dinner. Something a little nicer than a burger joint."

"The condemned woman gets a last meal?"

He winced.

"I'm sorry," Sarah said. "It's just I feel like I've got this sword of doom hanging over me and it's going to fall soon. But I'm not going to mention it again this evening. Promise. And I'd love to get some food that hasn't been kept warm under lights."

"A glass or two of wine would help us both calm down," he added. "Let's agree not to talk about it during dinner. We need a time-out. A break."

"Done."

During the meal, Jay regaled her with stories from his youth, pranks he and his brothers played and adventures from his college days. She recognized the effort he put into entertaining her, to divert her thoughts from the ugly realities of her situation. For the most part he succeeded. At times he had her laughing so hard her side hurt. His parents had had their hands full with their rambunctious sons.

"They did a good job of raising you. Your parents should be proud."

"I guess they are. They were a bit heavy-handed at times, but they did okay."

After dinner they drove a short distance to a plaza near downtown where they walked up and down the streets for a while. They didn't talk much as they strolled, hand-in-hand, looking into the display windows of storefronts. They ducked into a small place that served gorgeous desserts, where they each had coffee and shared a piece of divine chocolate cheesecake.

Then they walked some more. The crowds dwindled as the night wore on. Stores and shops closed. Most of the people moved into theaters or clubs or bars for the evening. A chill breeze blew. Jay's hand surrounding hers provided the additional warmth she needed beyond the jacket she wore.

Rooted in a solid understanding of each other, the silence between them provided a comfortable refuge from the emotional turbulence. Though it didn't offer any cure for her problem, the walking helped dissipate the anger and frustration closest to the surface. The stuff that would likely have kept her from sleeping or resting at all that night. Wrapped in the calming warmth of Jay's kindness, she slipped into a place where the hotter emotions banked to a low glimmer.

"We probably should be getting back."

Though she hated to hear him say it, he was right. The breeze had cooled enough to make them both start to shiver, and the hour was getting late.

When they were back in his car, he turned on the engine but hesitated before putting it in gear. "Your place or mine?" he asked. Nothing in his tone indicated he had any expectations about what would happen.

How did she decide? She knew what she wanted, but it wasn't fair to him. She hated creating more conflict for him. He had plenty already.

She sighed. "Mine."

His expression gave nothing away when he nodded and pulled out of the parking place. He drove in silence for a few minutes.

"Is that what you really want, or are you trying to protect me?" he asked.

"When did you take up mind reading?"

His small grin held more wry sadness than amusement. "It's not exactly mind reading. More like I'm beginning to understand what makes you tick. You're very protective of the people you care about."

"To a fault?"

He shrugged. "Most people would say no. I'm not sure it's entirely good for you. But it's an ingrained habit by now, I'd guess."

She hadn't ever thought about it that way but conceded he had a point. "You don't want me to protect you."

"From myself? No. I can handle that on my own. And make my own decisions about what I need to be protected from."

"Then let's go to your place. I'd feel safer there. And right now, there aren't many places I can say that about."

"If you're sure."

"I'm not sure of much of anything." She had so many questions and so few answers. "Jay, when you married Theresa… Were you in love with her?"

He didn't answer until he'd negotiated a tricky left turn. "I thought I was. But I have some of that same problem with protective instincts, and she appealed to those. In her case, I think I was more in love with the idea of having someone need me that much than I was with her. Sam says I have a tendency to rescue waifs and strays."

"I guess I kind of qualify in that category."

"Not hardly." He pulled into a parking place at his apartment complex. "It's one of the things that appealed to me about you. You refused to play the poor-me card or go for inspiring pity. Every time life beats you down, you pick yourself up and get up swinging, ready to try again. You make the best of whatever you have, without asking for help or handout. You keep trying to rebuild, using whatever you've got. You have to be one of the strongest, smartest, most inspiring people I've met."

"Wow. I feel my head swelling. I've never thought of myself that way. In fact, I've never thought I was very strong or very smart at all. To me it's always just been doing what I had to, to survive."

They walked up the steps to his apartment. Once inside, he took her jacket and hung both hers and his in the closet. He removed the shoulder harness with holster and gun he wore beneath it and put it on a top shelf. "Do you want a drink?"

"No." Sarah wanted something else entirely from him. Himself. To share love with him, if only just this once. She wanted to know what sex felt like with a man she loved rather than with one she only sort of liked. Given the future she faced, this might be her only opportunity. "I just want you." She took a step closer, more than a little stunned by her audacity. Was this what desperation did to a person? But what did she have to lose?

He sucked in a sharp breath even as he reached out to fold her in his arms. "Sarah, I can't--"

She put a finger on his lips to quiet him. The sensual feel of his mouth sent shivers through her. "Don't worry. There won't be repercussions as long as you have protection?"

He nodded.

"Good. No strings. No hard feelings. No obligations. No further expectations as a result. No one else will ever know about it unless you tell them. I promise. I may not have tomorrow, so dammit, I want to have today. Kiss me, please. The way you did two nights ago."

Worry shadowed his beautiful light eyes as he stared down at her. It dug tight lines around his mouth and nose.

"Don't make me beg," she said. "Please?"

Finally, he nodded and led her down the hall to his bedroom. He drew her down onto the king-sized bed, on top of the quilted coverlet.

With an arm around her shoulders, he leaned her back while at the same time kissing her cheek and the side of her throat. Prickling warmth followed where his lips brushed her skin, spreading the excitement through her. His mouth found hers and the warmth inside turned to heat. This was what she'd missed in her single previous relationship. The volcano of need that began simmering whenever he was close, when he touched or kissed or stroked her skin.

He worked his hands under her sweater, pushed it up, and took his mouth from hers long enough to pull the knit fabric over her head. She twisted so he could reach the catch on her bra.

His breath caught on a sharp intake as he stared at her breasts. "You're beautiful, Sarah."

He covered them with his hands. Rough palms brushed over her nipples and she jolted with the unexpected, sharp sensations that shot through her.

She shifted closer and tore open the buttons of his shirt. When she got down to his waist, she stopped and pushed her fingers into the gap to rest them on the warm, hard flesh of his chest. Hair rasped under her palm. A sudden mad need to see more of him possessed her. She jerked the shirt aside. He yanked the bottom out of the waistband of his pants and shrugged it off his broad shoulders.

"You're beautiful yourself." She stared at his strong chest. A smattering of hair roughened the skin between his nicely defined pectoral muscles and narrowed as it followed the midline down to his waist.

"Men aren't beautiful. We're rugged, strong, handsome if necessary, but not beautiful."

"Strong, hard muscle *is* beautiful, and you have lots of it." Though his body tended more toward lean than bulging muscle, still he was firm and strong, with warm, sleek skin covering the work-hardened sinews.

"You say the nicest things to me."

She loved the feel of his flesh, the rumbling groan that emerged when she rubbed his chest, the sudden gasp and jerk as she brushed over his firm nipples.

He shifted until his head loomed over hers. His dark hair slid over her skin when he lowered his head and put his lips on her breast. He licked over her nipple, and sparks of light crashed into her. She moaned as his tongue brushed over the sensitive tip and shifted to the other breast. Every muscle in her body tightened, need rousing deep inside, a desire to have him closer, against her, filling her.

After he unbuttoned her pants and lowered the zipper, she slithered out of the garment, careful of her bandaged knees. Shivers chased up and down her spine when he slid her panties down her legs with maddening care and delicacy.

Just the feel of his gaze resting on her most private area pushed the heat and pressure inside her up another notch. He slid a hand up her thigh and gently touched between her legs. Shocking shards of sensation tore into her gut and worked their way deep into her core. She nearly jumped off the bed.

He jerked back and frowned. "Are you all right? Should I stop?"

She found her breath. "I'm fine. Better than fine. And don't you dare stop."

He cocked his head to the side and his eyebrows rose. "You've never been touched like that before?"

"No."

"Vince wasn't much of a lover, then."

"He did the best he could. But he wasn't a young man, and he was already having trouble with his health." Loyalty made her choose her words with care. "Having sex wasn't always easy for him."

Jay brushed a loving hand up and down her inner thighs, making her squirm and gasp. "He had trouble getting ready or staying ready. So when he could, you had to do it quickly?"

She reached down and sifted through the smoothness of his straight dark hair. She loved the soft slide of the strands between her fingers, the warmth of his skin, his intelligence and understanding. She loved everything about him. "Yeah, pretty much."

"He could still have spent some time giving you more pleasure."

"He probably would have, but the effort always left him kind of wrung out. And it didn't matter to me all that much anyway."

"It didn't?"

"I liked him. I didn't love him...that way."

She levered herself up far enough to reach for the waistband of his pants, unfastened the button, and lowered the zipper carefully. Too carefully for him. He took over and jerked the tab down then stood up to let the trousers drop to the floor. He pushed the boxers down his hips as well, showing off an impressive erection.

"You're bigger than Vince," she said.

He settled back on the bed beside her. "It'll fit."

"Be kind of funny if it didn't."

"I don't know that *funny* is the word I'd use."

She reached down and wrapped her hand around his shaft. He drew in a sharp breath and his eyes shut tight, face screwing up in a tense response to her touch.

"Sarah! God..."

The erection felt huge to her. She worked her fingers up and down, reaching farther a couple of times to cup his heavy balls, exploring the unique masculine feel of him. Such an interesting contrast of hard and soft places.

His breath heaved in and out on harsher pants and his muscles tightened as she explored his body. He gently pushed her back on the bed and kissed his way from her lips down to her ear, along her throat, skimming her chest, taking a detour to visit each nipple, continuing across her stomach and abdomen until he reached her slit.

Only he didn't stop there.

She moaned when he kissed along the sensitive skin between her legs, seeking out the secret places, until she felt taut as a stretched rubber band and trembled with need.

"Jay, please." She didn't know exactly what she begged for, but somehow she knew he had the answer.

Before she finished the words, he had moved and nudged her legs apart. He reached over to grab a packet from a drawer in the night stand, rolled on the condom, crouched between her legs, and let himself down onto his elbows. He positioned himself to enter her, nudging at the opening. When she reached up to cup his cheeks in her hands, he smiled at her and pushed in.

He was so much bigger than Vince, he stretched her as he buried himself deep inside. He probed places Vince had never touched and ignited flares of pleasure like nothing she'd ever experienced. She jerked and groaned. Thrills chased up and down her body. Sparks exploded into agonizing excitement. She couldn't hold so much raw bliss. She wrapped her arms around his shoulders when he leaned down to kiss her again, possessing her completely. The man--this man--gifted her with sensations that lifted her right out of herself.

He pumped in and out, each stroke increasing the glorious pleasure and tightening her muscles more and more. Her body strained toward something spectacular.

"Sarah, you're so hot...and tight," he said between harsh panting breaths. "I can't make it last...longer."

His muscles felt like iron beneath her fingers.

"Don't need to." A volcano rumbled inside her, almost ready to blow with seething rapture building to unbearable intensity.

He looked into her eyes, and then he shut his, pulled almost all the way out, and froze for a moment before he slammed home inside her again. Something exploded within, the volcano erupting. Spasms jerked through her. Her panting breaths sounded a lot like sobs. The earthquake rolled and rumbled along every nerve until exhaustion wore it down.

Jay let out a long moan and sank down, resting his head in the hollow of her neck, undaunted by the aftershocks that jolted through her.

She wanted to stay there forever, basking in a peace and closeness like nothing she'd ever known. She stared at his face, so handsome, so strong, so tender. She wished she could stay in this moment forever.

But after a while, he slipped out and rolled to his side, taking her with him as he turned. She ended up closed in his arms with her back to his chest.

The warmth was real, the comfort and safety an illusion, but they all felt equally wonderful. For a while she could bask in it and have it to treasure later.

A time was coming, probably all too soon, when she'd need some good memories to cling to.

Chapter 13

Jay roused as the first light of morning poked through the slats in the blinds. Sarah muttered something and shifted without waking. He loosened his hold to let her settle again and then he watched her as she slept.

Near-black hair fell in tangled waves around her face and shoulders, while long lashes lay in graceful fans on her cheeks. Shadows bruised the hollows beneath her eyes. Despite the great sex, she'd hadn't fallen asleep right away. He'd felt her irregular breathing and the tension that remained in her muscles.

If only he could figure out a solution.

He shut his eyes while a wave of frustrated anger rolled through him. More than anything in the world right now, he wanted to protect her, and he couldn't do it. Just as he hadn't been able to protect Theresa. Sarah's demons weren't the same as Theresa's, but he felt just as helpless and frustrated in the face of them. It made him more than a little crazy that he loved her so much and could do so little.

He'd racked his brain for any clue they'd missed, any lead they'd failed to follow. He and Sam had chased an entire flock's worth of wild geese in search of answers and come up with nothing.

A pincer movement of danger closed in on her from either side. On the one hand, the pressure to make an arrest in the Capelli murder would victimize her if they couldn't track down the killers soon. And the killers themselves had apparently moved on from trying to find what she had to eliminating any possibility she might ever figure out what it was.

Sarah shifted again and opened her eyes. The slow, sweet smile was the most beautiful thing he'd ever seen.

"Lover," she muttered huskily, reaching for him.

The blood raced straight to his groin when her silky hair brushed his chest as she hid her face against him.

After a minute, she pulled back. "What time is it?"

"Early. We don't need to rush, especially not if you decide to stay here."

"Stay here?" Her eyebrows arched in a questioning look.

"It's the safest place for you."

"Oh. You mean like hide out here."

"That's what I mean."

"Until you have to arrest me. Then there's no place to hide, and I wouldn't, anyway."

"Would you run?"

"Like decide to get out of town instead of getting arrested?" She stayed quiet for a couple of minutes. "Where would I go? And how would I live? I don't think I could do it. And it would just make things worse when they...when you caught up with me."

"True."

"I'm not going to hide either. I'll be as careful as I can be, but hiding out doesn't solve anything, and it could cost me too much."

He tightened his hold on her. "I'm going to try to get someone to keep a watch on you. I doubt I can do it through the department. We're chronically short-staffed, but it doesn't hurt to ask. If that doesn't work out, we might hire a private bodyguard."

She giggled. "That would be so weird, to have my own bodyguard. I can see dragging him to class with me or into the library to sit there and watch while I study."

"If that's what it takes to keep you safe."

"I'm going to be very careful. Always walk with groups of other people, stay inside after dark--unless I'm with you--try not to drive any place lonely, and keep my doors and windows locked while I'm at home."

He sighed. "It's ripping me up that there's not more I can do. I should be doing something--anything--but I don't know what."

"You're doing something very helpful right now."

"I am?"

She nodded. "Fulfilling a dream. Making me feel like a fairy-tale princess when the handsome prince notices her. Showing me what it's like to be in love and to make love."

"Sarah, I--" He had no idea what to say to that.

"It's all right. You've given me some great memories. And if it's still pretty early, we have time to make a few more."

Her hand slid down his chest and along his abdomen. His erection rose to greet her fingers as they approached. And for the next hour they made some pretty nice memories. Memories he'd cherish as much as she did.

Making love with Theresa had never been like this. When she'd been alert enough to realize what was going on, she'd been greedy for the pleasure and the temporary respite from the pain of her existence. Other times, she'd acted like it was an unpalatable duty, necessary only to keep him satisfied and attached to her. If she even cared whether he enjoyed it, it never showed. And she'd never attacked him with such joyous and unselfish abandon as Sarah did.

When Sarah finally rolled over and said she needed to get going, he had to fight himself to let her. He told her so. She leaned over to kiss him once before she headed to the bathroom. Moments later, he heard the shower running.

An hour later they set out to her apartment again. "Your instincts are good about trying to stay safe," he said. "But the key thing is to never let down your guard. Don't assume you're okay just because there are people around. Or you don't see anyone threatening. You never know where the danger could be coming from so you have to stay alert all the time."

"I'll try."

"Good. And keep the cell phone in reach at all times. Is my number on speed dial? Good. Punch it if you even suspect trouble. Promise me?"

"I promise." She got out of the car and waved goodbye to him.

He hated to let her out of his sight, but she was an adult and she'd promised to be careful. Even if the caveman in him wanted to drag her back to the hearth and make her stay by the fire, the grown man and law enforcement officer knew she had the right to make her own decisions and do as she wanted.

* * * *

When Jay arrived at work at two that afternoon, Sam was already at his desk, and his demeanor gave the first clue something was wrong. Jay assumed the morose attitude resulted from their lack of progress in the case or from his unscheduled early departure yesterday, for the second time in a week. He was wrong.

Sam turned around to face Jay as soon as he'd settled at his desk. "Your girl's got a problem. A big one."

"I know. Someone tried to kill her yesterday. Probably the same people who killed Capelli."

"Not what I meant." Sam grabbed an envelope from his desk. "Capelli's family brought these in yesterday. Found them in a hidden drawer in his desk, or so they claimed." He handed the plain nine-by-twelve manila envelope to Jay. It bore no markings at all and hadn't been sealed, though the metal tabs showed creases where they'd been bent.

Jay shook it gently, letting the contents slide out into his hand. Three eight-by-ten-inch photos landed on his palm, but the image on the top one slammed into his gut like a sucker punch.

It showed Sarah smiling at an attractive young man on a sidewalk in front of a brick building, probably somewhere on the campus of the community college. The man stared back at her with a yearning expression. It had a date stamp in the lower right hand corner from the previous May. Jay spread the pictures out on his desk, touching them only on the edges.

"Evidence has been over them," Sam told him. "They got a couple of partials from both Dan and Marc Capelli. Maybe a couple of their father's, too, but there wasn't enough of those to be positive."

The second photograph showed the same two people, but in a deserted corner of a building where a wing met the main hall. The two stood close together, arms wrapped around each other. The young man faced away from the camera, but his clothes and dark hair matched the man in the first picture. Sarah stood between him and the building. The man was kissing her, holding her tight against him. Her hands rested on his arms.

The third picture made him suck in a sharp breath.

The date stamp said it was the same day. A couple lay in bed, the man's body atop the woman's. The picture showed the full length of them and both were nude. Dark hair and curve of cheek marked the man as the one in the other pictures. Only part of the woman's body showed--legs, one arm, a portion of breast and the side of her face. The cheek and the long dark hair belonged to Sarah. Jay picked it up and brought it closer.

"It's a fake," he said. "Photoshopped."

Sam's eyebrows rose. "How do you know?"

"There's just something...wrong about this."

"Wrong, as in that's your girl under another man?"

Anger made his blood start to fizz in his veins. "No. Wrong as in this woman has Sarah's head, but I'm not convinced that's her body."

"How much of an expert are you? Sam asked.

"Enough."

Sam's eyebrows shot up. "It's going to be the nail in the coffin as far as the sergeant's concerned."

"What's the chain on these? You said the Capellis brought them in? Anybody there when they were discovered?"

"Oh, yeah, those guys aren't that dumb. The drawer was found by an antiques dealer they had looking over the furniture. The brothers claim they knew nothing about it until the dealer showed it to them. I've checked with the dealer and he verifies the story."

"Easy enough scenario to set up. Has evidence gone over the desk?"

"Still waiting on their report," Sam said, "but it probably won't be much help."

"No."

"You know what this means."

"They're desperate. This could be our break. I've thought the whole set-up too pat. The older Capelli son, especially, looked like the type to want in on daddy's business. Or to want the whole block of wax if he and dad disagreed on...whatever."

"May be true, but that wasn't what I meant."

"Oh. You mean Sarah."

"I'm working on the paperwork for the arrest." Sam studied him with a sympathetic expression. "You want to tell her?"

"But why--? They're faked. At least that last one is."

"Can you prove it?"

Jay stared at the picture of the couple on the bed. His stomach twisted into a knot. "No. But I'll bet a photo expert could."

"And I'm sure her lawyer will have one examine the pictures."

"Graham knows about these?"

"The Capellis went directly to him. Not taking any chances on us," Sam said. "He's talked to the D.A. and they're going ahead with the case."

Jay sighed. "It's going to crush her."

"And you?" Sam stared at him intently. "Are you going to be a cop on this or a boyfriend?"

Jay ran his fingers through his hair and rubbed his scalp to relieve some of the tension. "I thought I'd have more time to get ready for it."

"Sorry, but time's up."

"Yeah." Jay sighed. "I have to be a cop. I can help her more as a cop than as a boyfriend."

"Jay." Sam's tone was harsh. "If you're going to be a cop, you can *only* be a cop. Not a boyfriend. Not even a friend. Just a cop."

"I know. She's going to think I betrayed her."

"Eventually she'll understand. She'll realize why you had to do it."

"Maybe. But maybe I really am betraying her."

"You're trying to do what's right. If she's the woman you think she is, she'll understand that. Maybe not at first. But eventually."

"I hope so." Despite Sam's reassurance, Jay didn't feel good about the decision. It felt wrong and dangerous and small, somehow. "I'm not even sure I'm doing it for the right reasons."

"I am."

"What? Sure? But if--?" He didn't even dare form the words. The thought was a gnawing beast in his gut.

"She's convicted? Then you'll do everything humanly possible, fight with everything you have, to find the truth."

"Actually, I was thinking worse than that. What if she really is guilty?"

"Wouldn't you rather know?"

"I don't know." He ran his fingers through his hair. "Yeah. I'd want to know. But she isn't. I have to believe that."

"And act like she is."

Jay nodded. "Can I bring her in? I'll arrange to meet her at her apartment after she finishes with her classes."

Sam took the pictures back and set them aside. "Don't see why not." His expression changed and got thoughtful. "You're right, though. It could be a break. They're getting desperate. They want something from her or they want to stop her finding it. Their initial frame-up didn't work. They tried to kill her and failed there, too. They plant additional evidence to ensure we arrest her. They found out lack of motive was the big hang-up. Solution: provide a motive. They want her out of the way badly."

"So we keep her in jail where she's safe."

"Actually I was thinking just the opposite."

"Dangle her as bait?"

"I'm thinking it's our best shot." Sam ignored Jay's outrage. "But here's the thing. It's got to look like everyone has abandoned her--you included. That means you have to back off and stay away."

Jay's stomach twisted. "We can't just leave her alone if we're going to do that."

"Who said we would? But it can't be you."

"Why not?"

"We have to let it look like she's totally on her own to lure them out."

"I can keep a low profile." Jay stared at his desk, but he still saw the images on those photographs in his head.

"You have to keep a profile of the professional cop going about his job."

"We're not going to leave her unprotected."

"Of course not. We hire private security. Not going to be cheap."

"Worth every penny, if it works. But if it doesn't?"

"How much worse off are you?"

"There's that. But I still don't like it." Jay wished the words hadn't sounded so petulant.

"Don't blame you. But what else have we got?"

Jay couldn't argue with that. He made the call to Sarah to set up the meeting. He didn't tell her why he was coming. When he considered how this was going to look to her, he felt like something that should be crawling along the ground, not walking upright.

* * * *

The call sent joy twisting through her. Jay wanted to meet her after classes. What they would do that evening? Before the sex, of course. Last night she'd experienced something she'd only read about in books and occasionally dreamed about.

His call had come while she was in the library after her last class. She hadn't studied as much as she should have for next week's exams and was trying to make up for it. She ran outside to take the call.

Since he wouldn't meet her for another hour, she went back to reviewing notes. Her mind refused to focus on English poetry.

After a while, she gave up on studying and headed home. As she walked across campus toward the parking lot, she reminded herself to stay alert. She watched other people around her. At the stairs that went down the hill to the parking lot, she rushed to catch up with a group of three students approaching the road where she'd almost been hit yesterday.

Staying right behind them, she made it to her car without incident.

Excitement bubbled through her at the thought of seeing Jay and spending time with him. Could another night ever equal what had happened last night? Probably not. That was magical. But it could be good. Really good.

She got home with twenty minutes to spare, so she changed into a nicer sweater to wear with the black jeans and reapplied her makeup. The buzzer at the door sounded while she brushed her hair out.

Excitement almost made her forget to look out through the peephole before answering, but she did and saw Jay standing there.

"You're early," she told him. "I was just--"

His expression stopped her. Hard and cold, it reminded her of the night of the murder, when he'd questioned her so harshly.

"What is it? What's happened?" Icy curls of fear twisted through her.

"Sarah, I'm sorry, but this isn't a social call. I've come to arrest you."

Chapter 14

She heard him, but the words seemed to come from a distance. She'd known it would come, had told herself she was ready. She wasn't. And not now. "I have midterm exams next week. I can't miss those."

"Exams are the least of your problems."

"I suppose so." She didn't know if she believed it. She didn't know what she felt or knew or believed. Her brain buzzed, refusing to process the fact that the sword had fallen.

"Sarah?"

She looked up at him. She didn't know what she believed about him either. Yesterday... Yesterday he'd loved her. This morning, even, he'd loved her. Now he looked at her like he believed she had killed Vince. "What changed? Why are you doing this?"

"You'll find out. For now, though, we have to go."

She nodded. "Are you going to put handcuffs on me?"

His expression went harder. "Do I need to?"

"I told you I wouldn't run away. That hasn't changed."

"No, I'm not going to cuff you. You need a lawyer. You want to call one right now?"

"I guess I'd better." Her brain didn't want to work. "I have a number for a lawyer, but I don't know where... Oh, it was in the desk, but I don't think it was in the papers. It probably got thrown away." Now what?

"Who is it? I can get the number."

"I don't remember. Someone Marc told me about. Oh, I guess I can call Marc and get it."

Jay nodded. "Go ahead. At least if Capelli recommended him, he's likely to be good."

"He is. Marc said he was. But he's not cheap. He said that, too." Her hands shook as she pulled out the phone and pressed the speed dial button for Marc. He answered on the third buzz.

Sarah told him she was being arrested.

"I'll call Trent and ask him to get there as soon as he can," Marc promised.

She thanked him and ended the call. Looking around the apartment, she spied her backpack on the floor next to the computer desk. "Can I take my books with me?"

"I wouldn't," Jay said.

They probably wouldn't let her keep them. "Okay."

She got her purse and went with him to his car. He let her take the time to lock up the apartment and her car as well. They didn't talk on the way to the jail.

The next few hours passed in something of a blur. Jay read her rights to her, she signed some papers, and then he left her with strangers who acted like she was a bit of dirt that had to be swept up. She answered a bunch of factual questions about herself, her name, date and place of birth, social security number, lots of other numbers. They took her mug shot, she was forced to strip, searched, and they took her purse, giving her a receipt for it. She answered a bunch of questions about her health and medical issues. The whole process was unbearably humiliating and seemed to go on forever. Every time she thought it was finished, they found something new and even more embarrassing to make her do.

They put her in a small room with a locked door to wait for her attorney to get there. A very long wait. The walls seemed to close in on her periodically, making it hard to breathe.

After what seemed like hours, someone came to get her. Her wrists were cuffed before they proceeded down a number of hallways, making turn after turn, until Sarah was so completely disoriented she might as well have entered another world. Some fantasy realm where an ogre had her trapped in the bowels of a major cave fortress. They went down in an elevator, through more halls, up a set of steps and finally ended up in a small courtroom.

A tall distinguished-looking man came over and extended his hand. "Miss Martin? David Trent. Marc Capelli asked me to help you. He's filled me in on the circumstances. We'll talk more after this, but for now, when we go in there for the arraignment, you let me do the taking, okay?"

She nodded. "Thank you."

"I told Marc I'd take care of you. Let's go in. I understand the press will be here shortly."

She followed the lawyer into a small courtroom. A man sat behind a desk on a platform at the far end. Another group of men stood to one side.

They included Jay and his partner, Sam, and two men she'd never seen before. Jay looked up and met her gaze, but his expression didn't change. No love there. No warmth. No friendliness. Nothing at all. Her chest hurt. She couldn't bear it and looked away quickly.

The proceedings didn't take long. She let the lawyer speak for her for the most part. She listened when they read that she was charged with the murder of Vince Capelli. When asked how she pleaded, the lawyer responded for her.

"My client pleads not guilty."

The judge named a tentative date for trial.

Trent and one of the men who'd been with Jay and Sam, who turned out to be the prosecutor, did some wrangling over bail. The judge finally set it at fifty thousand dollars. More than she had. A lot more than she could scrape up.

Then it was over, and the same people who'd escorted her there took her out of the room again. Before they left, David Trent told her someone would take care of bail, but it might take a little while. He'd arrange to talk to her more later.

She didn't look at Jay again. Mercifully, he left the room ahead of her. She realized why when they went out the door and plunged into a crowd gathered outside. Flashes went off as reporters took pictures. Others yelled questions, some at her, more at the police officers around her. A microphone almost hit her face as it was pushed toward her. She ignored it all, trying not to look at anyone or anywhere but straight ahead. Jay, Sam, and several other uniformed officers held the crowd to let her pass.

They took her to a block of cells this time and finally put her in one that had two sets of bunk beds.

Her escort pointed to the lower one on the left. "Yours." she said, before removing the cuffs, locking the door, and leaving again.

Two other women already occupied the room.

Sarah looked around at the small spare cubicle. It held only the two sets of bunk beds, plus a commode and sink in the corner. Neither had a screen or anything to offer privacy.

A large dark-haired woman stared at her from the far wall. "What're you in for?"

Sarah drew a deep breath to steady herself. "Murder."

The woman's brows rose. "Oh. Yeah? Who'd you kill?"

"No one. But they're saying I killed my lover."

Both women laughed.

The smaller woman sat on the lower bunk opposite hers. "Ain't no guilty people in here," she said. A lined face and faded blond hair spoke of a hard life. "Me, I didn't rob nobody, like they said I did. I just did some *borrowing*."

They laughed again.

"And I weren't dealing no drugs," the darker woman said. "They just got planted on me. I'll tell the judge that and he won't pay me no mind anyway. They already think they got it all figured out." The woman shrugged. "'Fraid you missed dinner. Not that you missed much. Damn vegetable soup again. You got any cigarettes on you, girl? I want one in the worst way."

"Sorry. Don't smoke. And they took everything I had."

"Yeah, you gotta work other channels to get stuff. This your first time, isn't it?"

Sarah nodded. "Probably be the last time, too, since they're likely to convict me of the murder."

"C'mon, girl, you gotta get a better attitude. It's your first time. They won't come down so hard on you." The lights blinked twice. "Oops. That's our sign. Lights out in ten minutes. You got business, take care of it now."

Once it was dark in the area, Sarah lay on the hard, lumpy mattress. Sleep refused to come. She didn't believe the dark-haired woman that they wouldn't come down hard on her. It was a high-profile case and a first-degree murder charge. She'd be fighting for her life.

Her mind roiled with the events of the day. Hard to believe it had started out with her and Jay making love that morning. Making memories. Good memories, but they didn't bring her any comfort now. She wasn't sure they were real anymore.

Even here in the jail bunk, she couldn't quite make herself believe she'd actually go on trial for murder. She didn't do it, so she shouldn't be tried for it. But she *had* done it, at least in the most physical sense of the word "kill." Her finger had fired the shot even if her will hadn't dictated the action. And that was the evidence that would convict her. The only fingerprints on the gun were hers. She'd told the cops she'd held the gun and her finger was on the trigger.

Would they ask for the death penalty? How could she face that? Cold chills poured down her spine. Nausea roiled her stomach and made her roll over, struggling to keep from being sick. This couldn't be happening. What had she done wrong that God or fate or whoever had charge of things did this to her?

How could *Jay* have done this to her? How could he be so loving one day and so cold the next? What made him change so drastically? Unless it had been an act from the very beginning. Maybe he'd played the caring, concerned lover to win her confidence and get her to confess. Or to stay close to her in case something gave away her guilt. He must have laughed inside when she told him he'd do the right thing when the time came. That hurt too much to think about for very long. He was the first man she'd ever really loved.

And likely he'd be the last.

She'd stayed in control for a while, telling herself she wouldn't give in and cry. But no one could see it now and the emotions overwhelmed her. She couldn't hold back the tears any longer.

She cried for a long time, trying to keep it silent, rubbing her eyes and nose on the thin sheet. Eventually she slid into a restless sleep.

* * * *

"We've got a problem," Sam said. He'd been on the phone for half an hour since they'd gotten back from the arraignment. "I've called every cop I know who does security detail on the side. Some major celebrity is doing a pair of shows at the arena on Friday and Saturday and they're bringing in all sorts of extra security. Everyone I've tried has already committed to that show."

"Crap. We've got to get some kind of protection for her. Whoever's behind Capelli's murder is getting desperate." Jay looked up security services in the phone book. The first two agencies he called couldn't help him. All their people were booked for the celebrity shows. The third one said they might have someone available. They'd have to check and get back to him. Jay tried several more with no success.

While he was considering and rejecting alternatives, his phone buzzed. The third agency he'd tried said they had a candidate for him to consider. The man was older, nearing retirement age, and couldn't stand for very long. He could do routine surveillance and monitoring, as long as he could do it mostly from his car.

With no other good choices available, Jay said he'd have to do and made the arrangements. Ben couldn't start until noon the next day, however.

Jay got the man's cell phone number and gave them his own.

* * * *

The lights flared on, jolting Sarah out of a strange dream of running in the woods with some unknown monster chasing her.

"Rise and shine, sunshine," the dark-haired woman said. "You don't get to lay in around here."

Someone came to the cell shortly to herd them into a communal shower where she stood with a dozen other women under jets of lukewarm water and washed with hard soap. They passed around a harsh lemon-scented shampoo. At least they each got fresh jumpsuits once they finished.

Breakfast came to the cells on trays. Each held a box of corn flakes, containers of milk and orange juice, two sugar packets, a cup of barely lukewarm coffee, a napkin, and a plastic spoon. Sarah couldn't work up any appetite for the cereal. She drank the orange juice and tried the coffee. It was worse than the police coffee they'd given her the night of Vince's murder. She forced herself to drink it because she wanted the caffeine, but it was so weak she wondered if it had any punch at all.

Before she got through half of it, a female officer came to the cell.

"Martin?"

Sarah nodded.

"Come with me." The woman escorted Sarah to a small room and handed her the clothes she'd removed the previous night. "You can change in here. I'll give you ten minutes."

The woman disappeared again, closing the door, and Sarah stripped out of the orange jumpsuit, gratefully putting on her own jeans and sweater again. No mirror graced the cubicle, but she ran a comb through her still-damp hair to try to restore order.

"What's happening?" Sarah asked when the woman returned.

"Guess someone posted bail for you."

"Who?"

The woman shrugged. "Not my business. You'll find out shortly. Let's go."

Maybe Jay had relented or had a change of heart?

They returned her purse and made her sign a few more papers before they finally escorted her out to the front lobby area. She didn't see him waiting for her there. In fact, the only other person in the room sat behind the desk.

The clerk gave her some papers and an envelope.

"Your lawyer posted bail for you," the woman said. "He also left this. Said for you to use it to get home."

The envelope contained fifty dollars in cash. Sarah called a taxi. It was almost ten by the time she got back to her apartment. She might have gone on to campus, but she desperately wanted to shower again, to wash away the jail smell first.

She called David Trent after that and got his assistant.

"I'm glad you called," he said. "We need to set up an appointment for you to come in."

They worked out a time next Tuesday afternoon. Then Sarah asked, "I wanted to thank Mr. Trent for posting bail for me. I didn't realize lawyers did that for their clients."

"They don't," the assistant said. "Hold on. Let me check the case notes." He was quiet a moment, though she heard the clatter of keys being tapped. "Oh. It looks like someone posted bond through Mr. Trent. But he wants to remain anonymous."

Marc must have arranged for the lawyer. Likely he'd taken care of bail as well.

"Can you tell me why they arrested me now? They must have some new evidence I didn't know about."

The assistant tapped keys again. "We don't have much on your case yet, but it looks like there were some photographs. We'll request copies from the D.A.'s office. When you come in Tuesday we should know more."

Sarah thanked him and ended the call. She tried to call Marc, but got his voice mail. She left a message expressing her gratitude.

* * * *

Jay hadn't slept much. The look of horror and betrayal on Sarah's face when they'd brought her in for arraignment haunted him.

The orange jumpsuit emphasized her pallor, and dark splotches shadowed her eyes. He recognized the stiff expression she wore through most of the proceedings, the one that meant she struggled to keep her emotions in check. How humiliating had the whole arrest and booking process been for her? She'd never forgive him for putting her through that.

He might never forgive himself for it. Especially if he couldn't figure out who was really behind the murder, and she was convicted. Or she was hurt or worse because their security didn't take care of her well enough. That sheer agonizing possibility kept him tossing and turning until exhaustion finally put an end to it shortly before dawn.

He woke feeling groggy and unhappy with himself. His watch said eight thirty and he wouldn't be getting back to sleep. He'd arranged bail for Sarah, through her lawyer so it could remain anonymous, but the arraignment had been so late, she wouldn't get out until this morning, probably right around now.

A desperate urge to call her made him reach for his cell phone. He longed to hear her voice and to explain his actions. Before he could punch her number, though, he stopped himself. He had to stick with the plan. Mostly. Staying away wasn't an option since Ben couldn't get there until noon. Jay intended to keep watch himself, but stay out of sight.

First he had to get coffee. His head ached and his mind barely functioned. He needed caffeine.

After downing the first cup, he showered quickly, got some things together, and headed for his car. He arrived at Sarah's apartment complex by nine thirty and parked in an out-of-the way corner, where he could see her but she likely wouldn't notice him. Ten minutes later, a cab pulled into the parking lot and stopped in front of the building. Sarah got out, paid the driver, and went inside.

He wanted to follow her in but forced himself to stay in place. Would she try to make it to any of her classes? He waited, watching and drinking the coffee he'd brought in a travel mug, but she didn't come out again. At eleven thirty he called Ben to give him directions to the apartment complex and tell him where to park.

An old Chevrolet with a rusting body showed up at five minutes to noon and proceeded to the side of the building. Jay used his binoculars to study the man as he sat in his car. "Nearing retirement" had missed the mark by several years at least. His bulk provided more than enough explanation for his inability to stand long. Jay quashed his first impulse to call the agency back and tell them this guy wouldn't do. Until they could round up someone better, this was the only alternative to no protection at all.

Jay's first conversation with the man didn't improve his opinion. Ben wheezed as he spoke, and his reaction time to questions left Jay clenching his fists and reminding himself to stay in control.

He briefed the man as thoroughly as he could before he had to leave to get ready for work. While driving home to change clothes, he fought the urge to turn around and go back.

Jay walked into the office an hour later.

"Looks like you had a rough night," Sam said.

"What do you think?"

"I hope it wasn't as bad as you look."

"Think worse."

"Hell. Sorry."

Jay shrugged. "Didn't get any better this morning. The guy we hired to watch her is a loser. Near seventy and way overweight."

"We've got to do better than that. She's a target. Let me make some more calls. Maybe I could call in some favors."

"I can't help thinking I made the wrong choice. I should have stood by her. Yeah, I'd get suspended. Maybe fired. But at least I'd have the time to keep watch on her myself. And she wouldn't hate me. Anyway, she's the only way we're going to solve this case now. I can at least take time off tomorrow and do it."

"As long as you stay out of sight and make sure the sergeant thinks you're fighting some virus."

"If he finds out what I'm doing, you knew nothing about it. Understand? I'm taking a chance with my career. I'm not risking yours as well."

"Oh, hell. I'm planning to take my share of the credit when we crack this case. I'll take my share of the risk too."

"I mean it, Sam. I don't need that guilt too."

"Hey, quit it. I'm a big boy. I make my own decisions. You got that?"

The sergeant came into the room, interrupting the discussion.

Jay said a quick, "Got it," while their superior made his way toward them.

"D.A. wants to meet to talk about the Capelli case," he told them. "Twenty minutes. Bring everything you've got." The sergeant gave them each the kind of look that didn't need words to say, "You *will* be there." Then he turned and left.

"Guess I won't be lighting out right away." Jay tried to force himself to relax. "I'll have to hope Ben Gleason is good enough to keep tabs on her for the afternoon, at least."

* * * *

Sarah couldn't work up the energy to go to campus since she'd already missed two of the three classes she had on Fridays. Instead, she stayed in and tried to study. With the threat of a trial and possible conviction looming over her, she struggled to keep her mind on the books.

When her cell phone buzzed at quarter to three, hope that it might be Jay flared. She looked at the Caller ID and saw Marc's number.

"Sarah, are you okay?" he asked.

"As okay as you can be when you've spent the night in jail. But thank you for bailing me out."

The line went silent for a moment. "What makes you think I bailed you out?"

"The lawyer refused to tell me who it was, but I assumed it had to be you. Who else?"

Again he hesitated, though it was briefer this time. "Why not your cop friend?"

"My cop friend arrested me yesterday. Turns out he was only hanging around to get enough evidence to convict me."

"Crap, that bites. I'm sorry, hon. Listen, we need to talk about some things, like how to get you out of this. Would it be all right for me to come over? I'll bring pizza for supper."

"Sounds good."

The promise of help didn't make it easier to keep her mind on her studies, but she exerted her will and concentrated on the review.

Her doorbell buzzed at five-thirty. She checked through the peephole and saw Marc, holding up a pizza on his raised hand like a delivery boy. She got her first surprise of the evening when she opened the door to him. His brother Dan was with him, standing to one side, out of her line of sight through the peephole. A few alarm bells rang at his presence, but not strongly enough to make her slam the door on the two men.

"Come on in," she said.

As he entered, Dan handed her a bag that held a bottle of soda and a bottle of wine. "Take your pick what to serve." He didn't openly sneer or frown at her, but she couldn't read anything else in his expression.

"Let's eat it while it's hot," Marc said.

Sarah got out her few matched dishes and cutlery and set the small table Jay had given her. She wouldn't think about that last part. It hurt too much. The table and chairs had escaped the worst of the vandals' damage. The three of them shared the bottle of soda since Sarah said she needed a clear head for her studies.

Over dinner, Sarah filled them in on the arrest and the humiliation of the booking process and her night in jail. She even let herself vent a bit about her fear and frustration. "I don't know why they decided to arrest me *now*. Your lawyer's assistant said it had to do with some pictures, but I have no idea what he's talking about."

Marc shrugged. "You need to set up a meeting with Trent. I expect he'll tell you then."

"I have an appointment with him next Tuesday."

"Good."

"But I feel so helpless. All the evidence is against me, and I don't know what to do, how to prove I didn't plan to kill him. Didn't *want* to kill him."

"Yeah, that's gotta feel rough," Marc said. "The only thing you can do is figure out this 'key' business. That might be what you need to prove you didn't do it."

"Heck, I know that. If it were that easy, I'd have gotten myself out of it long before now."

Marc offered a thin smile. "Let's try to approach it logically. Maybe we can figure something out."

Sarah shrugged. "What can it hurt? But I've been trying for weeks now, and so have the cops."

"Let's think about it. A key. I feel sure you've looked at all the keys on your key ring more than once and you can account for all of them."

"You can't imagine how many times. And I only have three keys on my ring now, one for my car and two for this apartment, one for the regular lock and one for the deadbolt."

"You didn't have any keys for Dad's house?"

"I did, but the guys who tried to rough me up a couple of weeks ago took them. And I knew what each of them opened."

"And you've checked every secret hiding place possible? Any and every place you can think of where he might have hidden a key?"

"I have, the cops have, and some thugs who broke into the place earlier this week did. I haven't found it and the cops didn't either. The cops don't think whoever trashed the place found it."

"Why not?"

She explained Jay's reasoning about the extent of the destruction.

"Makes sense." Marc wove his fingers together and turned them inside out.

His brother studied her with an intensity that sowed a few seeds of alarm. Probably being arrested and spending a night in jail made her hypersensitive.

"So what's left?" Marc asked. "Things you didn't take with you from the house?"

"Seems safe to assume the cops went over the place pretty thoroughly, especially my room and my things."

"Okay, eliminate that. What's left? How about something you might have taken with you out of the house when you went with the cops?"

"Only my purse and the clothes I wore. I've checked the clothes, and I've been through my purse several times. I even tore out the lining-- it was a pain to fix, too--but no spare keys in there. Cops have looked through it, too"

"What if... What if it wasn't a physical key he gave you, but some information that could provide a key to...something?"

"We've thought of that too. I've looked through all my files and everything else I could think of."

He looked around the apartment. "Don't you have a computer?"

"A laptop. It's in my book bag. You think he might have put something on there? I think I would have noticed a file I didn't know about. And anyway, I'm pretty sure the police went through it, too."

"Still, we might notice something others would overlook." Marc nodded toward his brother.

Sarah went to the computer desk. She brought the book bag back to the table. She took her purse out of the top of it and pulled out the laptop. After unlatching it, she turned it on and let it boot up while she connected the power cable.

When it was ready, she said, "See if you can find anything."

For the next fifteen minutes, both brothers poked around in the Explorer Window, scanning file names, opening various things and discussing possible names for whatever they sought.

"It's not that one," Marc said. "That's just an essay on some English King."

"Henry the second," Sarah said. "For my English History class."

They ignored her.

"He might have called it something like 'exchanges,'" Dan ventured.

"Didn't see anything like that," Marc said. "Or anything with 'Wilson' or 'Cumbert' in the title."

Sarah grew increasingly uneasy. They seemed to have too good an idea what they might be seeking. Still... Of course they might. They'd known their father a lot longer than she had and knew a good bit more about his more secretive business.

How much more?

While they pored over files on the computer, she forced out a sneeze and pretended to search for a tissue in her purse. Using that as a cover, she snagged her cell phone, turned it on, found the number for Jay, but didn't press the call button. Would he even respond? She might be better off calling nine-one-one, but that could be iffy from a cell phone. She'd have to trust that, whatever he felt about her, honor would compel him to answer a distress call. Her fingers slid over her key ring and the little pen fob.

Finally Marc sighed, looked up, and shook his head. "Not here. Did Dad give you any disks or CDs? Anything he might have put a file on?"

"Not that I recall."

"Are you sure? Think, Sarah."

His insistence bothered her. It seemed too centered in something other than concern for her. "I'm pretty sure he didn't. He gave me a couple of DVDs, but they were pre-recorded so he couldn't put anything else on them. I think I left them behind anyway."

And then it hit her.

Vince hadn't given it to her, but he'd teased her about it, and he could have put a file on it. At the same she knew without a doubt she shouldn't tell the Capellis.

Unfortunately she didn't have good control of her face.

Marc looked up and saw something there. "What? You thought of something, didn't you?"

She racked her brain to come up with a convincing lie. "The DVDs. He might have put something in the liner notes."

"What's the relevance to a key?" Marc asked.

"Um…isn't there a key or something to a DVD?"

"You're lying, Sarah, and you're not very good at it."

"What?"

"You had a thought about the key Dad gave you."

"I just told you. A DVD."

"No." His tone declined from pleasant to menacing. "Sarah, I need to find that key. Need it very badly. So you really should tell me what you just thought of." His eyes and lips narrowed as his expression got hard and cold.

Her heartbeat picked up speed as fear sent icy tendrils along her skin. This wasn't the friendly Marc she knew. This man looked and sounded like someone who'd do nasty things to get what he wanted. *Think.* She sneezed and reached for a tissue again. Under cover of doing that she grabbed the cell phone and pressed the button to make the call. She flipped the phone over so it rested against the side of the bag to muffle the sound of it buzzing. "I… It's not anything. Just something I need to tell the cops about." She sneezed as loudly as she could a couple of times to cover any noise from the phone.

He stood up and moved until he loomed over her. "I think it's something you need to tell me about."

She barely heard Jay say, "Yes?"

Marc didn't seem to notice. His attention was focused entirely on her.

"Why? What's your interest?" Her voice wobbled.

His wry smile held no humor but a lot of threat. "I've told you, I want to help you get out of this mess."

She heard Jay start to repeat her name, a bit louder. To cover the sound, she raised her own voice. "By scaring me like this? Look, I had a thought, but it's not something that's going to help with this. Okay?"

"Not okay, Sarah."

She sneezed again and reached for another tissue, in the process turning the phone over and pulling it out a bit. The bag should still hide it from the men's sight, but she hoped Jay would hear what was happening. She looked up at Marc. "I just thought of an old friend of your father's who might know something about it."

Marc's eyebrow rose. "Who?"

"Tom Pettigrew."

She hoped the slight hesitation before she answered wasn't too obvious.

Apparently it was. "You're lying, Sarah, and I repeat--you're not very good at it." With startling speed and stunning viciousness, he swung a hand and slapped her face.

Stars danced at the periphery of her vision for a moment. Sarah stood up and backed away from him, angling toward the door and shouting, "Why are you doing this?"

Dan Capelli rose and planted himself firmly in her path. She tried to side-step around him and he moved to block her. She whirled as Marc grabbed her shoulders from behind.

"I need to know what you thought of a few minutes ago."

"Why do you need it so badly?" she asked.

"Let's just say that there might be some things secured by that key that would be...inconvenient for us."

"Your father had something on you?" She should have sounded shocked and disbelieving, but she didn't. She sounded cynical.

Marc shrugged. "The old man didn't appreciate some of our...freelance efforts."

"You killed him."

Marc shook his head. "Of course not. We just dropped a few words where they would scare someone into action."

"You killed him. Not yourself, but you set it up."

"You're too clever, Sarah. But it's irrelevant. We only want the key the old man gave you. So where is it?"

Dan didn't say anything. He just stood in her way, cold and expressionless, like a man doing a job he didn't love but didn't hate either. Doubt and worry turned into full-blown fear as she worked out the implications of Marc's words. She started to shake. God, she hoped Jay hadn't just hung up on her. The phone wasn't buzzing or anything. She needed to get out of there. Fast. But the apartment only had one door, and Dan Capelli stood in her way. Her stomach was doing flip-flops. She glanced around wildly, trying to find an alternative to the door. She'd never get a window open before they grabbed her.

She had a vague memory from a self-defense class. *Attack first and without warning.* She lifted her leg to sweep it around, trying to catch Dan on the knee with the side of her foot. It might have worked, but Marc saw it coming and dragged her backward by the shoulders. He turned her and roughly pushed her back into the chair she'd been occupying earlier, only now it was turned so that it faced out into the room, back against the edge of the table.

"Stay there," Marc ordered.

Dan loomed over her with narrowed eyes and a leer that suggested he might like it if she tried to get up.

Marc pulled something out of his pocket--a scarf. He'd come prepared for more than just pizza. She jumped up and tried to run, but Dan caught and held her. Between the two they forced her back into the chair. Marc yanked her arms around behind it, below the level of the table, and tied her wrists together with one of the scarves.

Cold blasts of terror poured over her. Even if Jay heard and recognized what was going on, he'd never get to her in time. Nausea roiled her stomach as she saw what Marc held when he straightened up.

The knife's blade had to be eight or nine inches long with a nasty curved point at the end. It gleamed with a wicked silvery shine.

"Now, Sarah, let's talk about that thought you just had."

Chapter 15

Jay forced himself to pay attention to the D.A.'s and the sergeant's words at the meeting, since they could prove important to Sarah. The case sounded stronger than he wanted to admit when they reviewed the evidence against her. Until they got to the potential weaknesses, especially the evidence that someone else *had* been in the house that night.

When his cell phone chirped he reached to turn it off. On impulse, though, he looked at the screen first. It showed Sarah's number.

He muttered, "I need to take this," to the others, and answered, "Yes?"

She didn't say anything. He heard muffled sounds in the background and what sounded like a man's voice.

"Sarah?" he asked, louder. It drew the attention of the others in the room with him.

Suddenly the noises on the other end weren't as muffled, though still well away from the phone. He heard a man's voice clearly enough to identify him as one of the Capellis, though he couldn't understand the words. A sharp clap preceded a squeal from Sarah. Jay's fists tightened. One of them might have hit her.

Then Sarah said, "Why are you doing this?" She wasn't talking into the phone but had shouted it loudly enough for him to hear clearly.

He waved a hand and then put a finger over his lips to signal everyone in the room to silence, upped the volume on his phone to max, and set it on the table just in time to hear Capelli say, "I need to know what you thought of a few minutes ago."

Sarah asked, "Why do you need it so badly?"

The room got so quiet he could hear everyone breathing as they listened to the conversation.

Jay's heartbeat ratcheted into high gear. He put his hand over the phone to mute it for a moment as he looked at Sam. "Get that moron of a guard and find out if she's still in her apartment and how those guys got past him."

Sam stood and hurried out of the room. Jay took his hand off the phone, and they all listened in stunned silence.

Sarah's voice said, "You killed him."

The man said, "Of course not. We just dropped a few words where they would scare someone into action."

Jay almost laughed at the looks of shock on the faces of the other men in the room.

"You killed him," Sarah repeated. "Not yourself, but you set it up."

"You're too clever, Sarah. But it's irrelevant. We only want the key the old man gave you. So where is it?"

He turned to the others and put his hand over the phone to mute it again while he picked it up. "There's your case, gentlemen. I've got to go." He drew a sharp quick breath, trying to calm the fear twisting his stomach into knots, stood up, and ran out to the hall where Sam spoke into his phone. Jay nodded for him to come along.

Sweat beaded on his forehead despite the cold chills running down his back. He couldn't get to the parking lot fast enough, especially when a thin squeal of fear came from Sarah. Sam spoke to the guard while they ran, then hung up and pressed in another number.

"She's still in her apartment. I'm driving," Sam insisted. "You stay on the line." He handed his phone to Jay as well. "I just dialed dispatch. Mute yours so they can't hear you and tell dispatch where to go. Then get the guard again."

Jay muted his phone with mixed emotions. He couldn't make any noise that would alert her captors to the open line. But he desperately wanted, needed, to know what was happening in her apartment. Or did he? Could he bear to listen while they frightened her or tormented her or-- Hell, it was possible. They might kill her. His breath clotted in his throat.

The dispatcher came on Sam's phone. Jay drew air in to clear the obstruction, identified himself, and asked for every available unit in the area to go to Sarah's place. "It could become a hostage situation," he warned. "Have them approach carefully."

"Will do," the woman said. "You want to stay on the line with me until they get there?"

"No, I'll call back to check on progress." He ended that call and dialed Ben's phone. "What the hell is going on there?" he asked.

"Nothing."

"The hell. Something's happening. Did you see anyone go in or out?"

"Nope. Just the pizza delivery guys."

"The *what*?"

"A couple of guys delivering pizza. Come to think of it, I don't remember seeing them get back in their car."

"Since when do guys deliver pizza in *pairs*?" He clenched his fists and exerted every bit of control he had to keep from yelling at the idiot. "Get in there and find out what's going on. But be careful. I don't want this to end up in a hostage situation or worse. We've got cops coming your way, too."

Sam had the blue light on his dash, but he hadn't turned on the siren. He wove through late rush-hour traffic on the highway.

"Can you pick it up a bit?" Jay begged.

"Not and stay alive. Call dispatch back and get an ETA for the nearest unit."

Jay followed his partner's orders.

"We have a unit that's less than five minutes away," the dispatcher told him. "Two more should be there within ten."

"Tell that first one I'll buy him dinner if he makes it in three. And tell them all to approach carefully. There's a potential hostage situation."

"You've mentioned that," she said. "I'm reminding them now. Do we need the hostage team?"

"Maybe. Alert them." He turned the sound up on his own phone until he could just hear, holding his hand over the microphone as he put the unit to his ear. Sarah made a sound halfway between a shriek and a groan.

A man's voice said. "You don't want to make me use this, do you?"

"No." That was Sarah, barely able to get the word out.

"It's nice and sharp. I don't want to hurt you. I've always liked you, even if you did supplant my mother. Not that I blame him for preferring you. Mother's not the easiest person to live with, and she certainly isn't as pretty as you. You want to stay pretty, don't you, Sarah?"

Jay's entire body throbbed with the need to take the man by the throat and beat him senseless. At the same time, he prayed for Sarah to hang on just a few minutes longer.

* * * *

Marc waved the knife in front of her face for several minutes that felt like hours.

This couldn't really be happening. The room spun around her until she took several breaths through her nose. She couldn't take her eyes off the shiny surface of the blade. Her breath heaved in and out on gulping gasps that sounded like sobs. Tremors shivered along her spine. "Marc, you can't do this."

He drew the knife down her arm, splitting the fabric of her shirt from shoulder to elbow and leaving a shallow cut on her skin. For a moment she felt nothing except the warmth as blood welled from the slice. Then the sting started.

"Don't tell me what I can't do." He slid the knife along the inside of her lower arm, again parting fabric and the top layer of skin.

Sarah squealed.

"Blood!" Dan said. "You didn't tell me you there'd be blood. You know I hate the sight of blood."

"Just don't look," Marc told his brother.

Her heartbeat roared in her ears as it pounded in time with the throbbing cuts. More pounding came from someone banging on her door.

Dan looked at it nervously.

"Ignore it," Marc said. "They can't get in."

He turned to Sarah and held the knife up to her cheek. When he pressed slightly it nicked the skin. A trickle of blood slid down her face.

"Marc," Dan said. "Stop it. I don't like this." He looked at Sarah, scanning the path of the blood down her face to throat, and swallowed hard. "Let's get out of here."

Another series of raps came from the door. An unfamiliar voice said, "Hey, who's in there? Open up!"

Marc's eyes hardened and he looked at Sarah again. The knife pointed at her other cheek. "It's going deeper this time. Tell me where it is."

"No." That came from Dan, who looked genuinely horrified.

Marc gave him an impatient wave. "You have as much to lose as I do."

"I don't like this. Doing this to a woman. It isn't right. And all the blood…"

"It's necessary."

"No it isn't."

The knocking on the door turned to an urgent beat. "Come on. Open up before I break it down."

"Marc, look at me."

Something in Dan's voice drew both Marc and Sarah to stare at him. She was too far beyond terror to find even the sight of a gun in Dan's hand much more horrifying. It pointed at his brother rather than at her.

"Stop it. We're leaving now."

Dan reached behind him and turned the deadbolt. Just as he began to undo the other lock, Marc charged at him. Caught by surprise, or maybe just unwilling to shoot his brother, Dan didn't react. Marc grabbed the gun from him, Dan reached for it himself and the two struggled over it for a couple of minutes while the man outside continued to pound on the door and yell to let him in.

Both Capellis had their hands on the gun. It flashed over their heads, and then was pushed down to the side and disappeared from her sight.

While they fought, Sarah wriggled her wrists, pushing and straining until the fabric binding them began to loosen.

Just as she freed her hands, an explosion roared through the room, bouncing off the walls and ringing in her ears.

The two men froze and Dan backed away, cursing at his brother. "You frigging shot me!" He stumbled to the wall and slid down it. He held a hand to his left side, just above the waist, but blood slid over his fingers and spread through fabric beneath.

The smell of the blood roused vivid memories of the night Vince had died.

Marc looked around wildly. The thumping at the door had changed from knocking to a whomping. The wood in the frame started to splinter, but it didn't give way.

Marc turned to her and pointed the gun at her face, keeping it trained on her as he approached. Something froze inside as she stared into its evil little eye. Using his left hand, he grabbed her right arm and dragged her to her feet. The gun prodded at her temple. Sarah had gone so far beyond terror now she felt almost numb. It actually helped her think.

Outside a new voice ordered, "Police officers. Open the door."

Sarah reached for her purse. Marc saw it, realized the cell phone was close to her hand. Without taking the gun from her head, he knocked the phone to the floor.

The newcomer repeated his demand that they open the door.

Marc's rapid breathing almost matched her own. Disembodied words came from floor level. So much else had distracted her, she took a moment to realize they emerged from her phone.

"Sarah?" Jay's voice said. "Talk to me." A pause and then, "Capelli? Are you there? The apartment is surrounded by the police. Let's talk."

Marc stood frozen for a moment. He prodded Sarah with the gun. "Pick it up, but don't try anything. I haven't got much left to lose here."

She bent down, grabbed the phone, breathed a quick "Thank you," into it, and handed it off to Marc, who put it up to his ear.

For a few minutes he just listened, and then he said. "Your girl's okay. For now. You want to keep her that way, you get everyone far away from my car and no one gets close to us when we come out. What? Oh, black Beemer. It's on the right side of the door about six spaces down." He listened for a while. "Hell, no, I won't."

They went back and forth for quite a while, with Marc listening, responding negatively, and then listening some more. After several rounds, Marc finally said, "My patience is running out. If you want your girl in one piece, you let me get out of here now. Otherwise, I'll have to start taking her apart, starting with the fingers. I have a nice sharp knife, as she already knows." He listened again for a few minutes. "You can talk to her, but I'll be listening, too." He handed the phone to her. "They want to talk to you."

Sarah took the phone and put it to her ear, but Marc grabbed her arm and leaned in so he could listen as well.

"Sarah, are you all right?"

Jay's voice was the most welcome sound she'd heard in the last several hours.

"For the moment. Yes."

"Thank God." He stopped to take a deep breath. "We're going to work this out. We've got a hostage negotiator on the way."

"I don't have time for that, Cop," Marc said into the phone. "She doesn't have time. Ten minutes. You decide to let us go in ten minutes, or she starts losing fingers."

Chapter 16

"Jay, please," Sarah said. "Let us get out."

"You don't want to get in the car with him. That's a dead end." His voice sounded thin and strained.

She had a glimmer of an idea--a very risky and dangerous idea. "I understand. But it'll be all right. You can handle it. Please do as I ask. We'll work something out. Can you trust me in this, at least?"

"Sarah, I-- Never mind. I'll see what I can arrange. Give me a couple of minutes."

The silence between her and Marc was so tense, even their breathing sounded unaccountably loud. Sarah heard her own heart pounding. A swish from the other side of the room drew her gaze that way. Dan had been sitting with his back to the wall, but he slid to the side and hit the floor with a thump. His eyes closed.

Finally Jay came back on the line. "We'll let you come out and clear a path to the car on condition you agree to let Sarah go once you're in it."

"No dice. I need her. You've got two more minutes before I take a finger."

Sarah almost doubled over as a wave of nausea struck.

"Jay," she said into the phone. "Please, do as he asks. We'll work something out. Promise."

He was silent for a moment. "All right. Give me Capelli."

She handed the phone over. Marc listened for a moment with the phone to his ear so she couldn't hear. Finally he smiled and said, "Okay." He turned to her. "In five minutes, we're going out."

They were probably the longest five minutes of Sarah's life. Each second lasted a year as they both stared at the second hand on Marc's watch sweeping around the face. Sweat dripped down the sides of her face and under her clothes, but she didn't dare wipe it away. Finally, the time ticked off.

Marc reached for the deadbolt, found it already off, and twisted the lock beneath the knob. "You're going out first," he said. "But I'll be right behind you with a gun pointed at your head. Don't forget it or try anything funny. My finger's feeling kind of twitchy. Open the door."

Sarah hesitated a moment before turning the knob and pulling the door open. A group of men and women, several in uniform, stood at the end of the breezeway. They looked alert, poised. A few held guns drawn or their hands hovered over their holsters. She scanned them but saw no familiar faces.

"Get out of here!" Marc yelled. "Back. Out."

"Do it." The order came from a man in uniform who stood in the center of the group.

The gathered officers retreated, most walking backward or sidling to keep an eye on them as they left.

"Go." Something round and hard prodded at the small of her back. Sarah walked out of the apartment and down the hallway. Her knees wobbled so badly she couldn't believe her legs stayed beneath her. Jay was right. She didn't dare get in the car with Marc. But neither could she make a move here in the tight confines of the hallway.

They stopped again at the single step leading down from the hallway to the walkway outside. Twilight had faded into almost complete darkness, but many of the police cars had left their lights on and a few portable units burned as well. Added to the glow from the pole lights in the parking lot, they provided plenty of illumination. People were gathered there, including the crowd held back by barricades in the parking lot and lines of officers on the grass. Most of her neighbors huddled in the group of civilians. The cops must have evacuated them.

Sarah scanned the clumps of people and finally found Jay almost directly ahead, about fifty feet away, standing next to Sam. She hesitated to look at him, fearful she'd see the cold, hard man who'd arrested her. When she met his gaze, though, she found agony and terror in his expression, along with a helpless rage that vibrated through his tense body. He had his gun drawn and leveled, waiting for a target.

Hoping Marc couldn't see her do it, she mouthed at him the words, "Be ready," trying to exaggerate it enough he could read her lips. She didn't know if he understood exactly what she said, but he nodded.

Recalling what Marc had said about the location of his car, she leaned toward the right, but he grabbed her arm.

The gun prodded her side. "This way." He yanked her toward the left.

The police had figured it out, since they'd retreated from the area she and Mark headed for.

She waited until they were about a third of the way across the grassy area between the building and the parking area, the most open and exposed place. She stopped and said, "Wait, I need to tell you something."

"What?" Marc said. Impatience made the word short and clipped.

She looked around and turned as much as she dared back to face Jay and yelled across the space. "My keys are on the table in the apartment. The little pen fob on it has a hidden flash drive. What do you want to bet the 'insurance' is on there?"

As she'd hoped, the revelation froze Marc into a moment of indecision. His grasp on her loosened just enough.

Sarah dove as far from him as she could, rolled on the ground, and scrambled in a mad crawl across the grass toward the nearest group of cops. A single gunshot was followed by several more. Sarah waited for the pain or shock of impact as she collapsed, panting, on the ground near a group of uniform shoes.

But the only blow came when a strong body almost crushed her to the ground and lay over her as a human shield.

She didn't know exactly when the shooting stopped. The echoes reverberated in her ears. The body on top of hers squashed the air out of her. She'd rather struggle to breathe than lose the protection. Relief poured through her, so deep and profound it had her shaking and close to tears.

"Are you all right?" Sam whispered in her ear.

"I think so."

"Is she okay?"

Sarah could barely turn her head enough to see Jay standing over them. He met her eyes and relief made his shine. "It's over. We've got an ambulance coming, but I don't think there's much they can do."

"Marc?"

Jay nodded and stretched out a hand to help her upright. "I'm sorry," he whispered to her. "Sorry for everything." He touched the nick on her face and his eyes tightened in pain.

"It's all right."

She had no time to say more before others gathered around them, asking how she was and congratulating Jay.

"That was a nice shot," an older man said. "How'd you get it off so fast?"

"Thanks, Sergeant," Jay said. "She told me she'd try something to get away, so I knew to be ready."

"She did?"

"I mouthed the words at him," Sarah said. "Thank God, you understood. You told me you were a good marksman. I was counting on that."

Jay put an arm around her shoulders and hugged her close.

Suddenly, Sarah remembered Dan. "His brother! Marc shot Dan. He's in my apartment." She started that way but Jay held her back. "Stay here with me. He'll be taken care of."

"I'm on it." Sam disappeared back into her apartment.

"Sarah"--Jay pulled her against him and held her tight--"I'm sorry for everything. Sorry you had to go through that. Sorry I had to arrest you and act like I didn't care. It half-killed me, especially knowing how it would look to you. But we thought it was the best way to draw out the real killers. Probably the only way. I know it was cruel. Can you forgive me for-- What the hell?"

He lifted his fingers from her arm and noticed the blood. Frowning, he lifted her arm and surveyed the damage. "He did this to you?"

She nodded. "He *really* wanted that file."

"File?"

"Computer file. I'm pretty sure the key was a computer file. Marc and Dan went over the files on my laptop and they seemed to have a pretty good idea what they were looking for. That was when I realized--"

"They'd organized their father's death. And we dangled you right in front of them," he said, his tone anguished. "Left you alone and at their mercy. I don't know if I'll ever forgive myself for that. We'd better get you to the hospital and get these cuts looked at. Sergeant!"

"Wait," Sarah said. "The flash drive. I want to find out if it really is the key. I didn't even think about it before because I never used it as a flash drive, but when they asked me about CDs or disks, I thought of it and remembered that Vince always called it a 'keychain drive.' He gave it to me a couple of years ago, and I haven't really thought of it since."

"Can't go back in there, hon," Jay said. "Your apartment's a crime scene again."

A pair of paramedics raced by them into her apartment. A few moments later, Sam came out.

"How is he?" Sarah asked.

"He'll survive. Good thing. We've got lots of questions for him."

"Sarah's flash drive might provide some of those answers," Jay said.

"When we can get to it. The SBI is almost certainly already on the way."

"I hope there's something useful on there." Sarah leaned into Jay's side, letting him support her.

"It almost doesn't matter now, anyway," Jay said. "You're clear."

"I am? How?"

He grinned. "When your call came in, we were in the middle of a meeting with the D.A., a couple of his people, and the sergeant. I turned the phone up when I realized what was going on, and every last person in that room heard what Marc said. Clever work, turning the phone on like that and dialing me without him knowing it."

"I was a nervous wreck. I was afraid if he knew what I'd done he'd kill me on the spot. Of course, I was pretty much figuring he'd do that eventually anyway."

"Sarah, I'm sorry. We had a guy on guard at your apartment, but obviously he wasn't worth much."

Sam explained that the guy was the best they could get under the circumstances. He, too, apologized for allowing her to be hurt.

"Speaking of which, I'm going to take her to the hospital to get this taken care of," Jay told his partner. "She won't be in any condition to answer questions until morning, and she'll be spending the night with me. The SBI can talk to us both tomorrow. Plenty of witnesses saw what happened."

Sam grinned and handed over his car keys. "Give me your gun for the SBI and get out of here quick before anyone sees you. Have fun."

Jay escorted her to a gray SUV and helped her into the front seat. The cuts on her arm throbbed, and she'd acquired a few bruises in her dive out of Marc's way. The astonishing relief of not having to worry about a trial and conviction for murder far outweighed those discomforts.

"There will still be some legal hassles involved in getting charges against you dropped and settling the case." Jay pulled out of the parking lot.

"Yeah, I figured. Still better than going on trial, though. Speaking of legal stuff--you posted bail for me, didn't you?"

"The lawyer wasn't supposed to tell anyone who did it."

"He didn't. But when I figured out it wasn't Marc, I knew it had to be you. How much did it cost you?"

He barked a harsh, humorless laugh. "A lot less than it's costing me to know you've been through hell in the last day or so and it was mostly my fault." He drew in and exhaled a long, slow breath. "Will you ever be able to forgive me?"

"There's nothing to forgive. You were doing your job as best you knew how, and trying the only thing you could to help me at the same time."

"I took a huge risk with your life. And I was damned careless with it. That's what I have the hardest time dealing with. I knew the guard we got was less than brilliant, but I rolled the dice he'd be okay until I could get the time off to keep watch myself or we could get someone better. That was almost a fatal mistake."

"Jay, pull over for a minute," she said.

He steered the car to the side of the street. The area was residential with plenty of parking available next to the curb. "Why?"

"So you can kiss me properly. Look, if there's anything to forgive, I forgive you. You've done your share of suffering for this too. Let's put it behind us now. We've a future to build."

He kissed her thoroughly, for a long time.

When he drew back, he said, "About that future. Do you think we could try to build it together?" The light from a nearby streetlight cast a sliver of radiance across his face, making his light eyes gleam. "I know I let you down once, but if you'll marry me, I promise not to let it happen again. And I know you don't need me. You're smart enough and brave enough to take care of yourself, but I need *you*. Desperately. I love you so much it hurts. You've given me back something that's been missing ever since Theresa died. I didn't even realize it until you came into my life."

Between relief that the shadow of a murder charge had lifted and joy that Jay really did care for her, Sarah wanted to laugh and cry at the same time. She wanted to sing, dance, and shout, but settled for putting a hand on his face. "Jay, I do need you. I can take care of myself, yes, and that's good to know. But you make me happy in a way I've never been happy before in my life. And you've never let me down. How many times have I called you for help the past few weeks? And you've always come. You even took the risk of letting it look like you'd betrayed me so that you'd be in a position to help. I admit I was hurt and angry for a while during that miserable night in jail, but I understand now why it was necessary. I love you, too. Always."

They spent the next few minutes kissing again, until he finally sighed and said, "We need to get you to the hospital."

"Okay. But first, what did I give back to you?"

He smiled, and the creases around his mouth and eyes melted her heart.

"You reminded me what it feels like to laugh."

Meet the author

Karen McCullough is a former computer programmer who made a career change into being an editor with an international trade publishing company for many years and now runs her own web design business. She is the author of more than a dozen published novels and novellas, which range across the mystery, romantic suspense, paranormal, and fantasy genres. She has won numerous awards, including an EPIC Award for fantasy, and has also been a four-time EPIC finalist, and a finalist in the Prism, Dream Realm, Rising Star, Lories, Scarlett Letter, and Vixen Awards contests. Her short fiction has appeared in several anthologies and numerous small press publications in the fantasy, science fiction, and romance genres. She lives in Greensboro, NC, with her husband of many years.

www.ingramcontent.com/pod-product-compliance
Lightning Source LLC
Chambersburg PA
CBHW022154260626
47155CB00018B/1931